MY FIRST
AND
LAST KISS

KAITLIN GATES

Copyright © 2021 Kaitlin Gates

All rights reserved. No part of this book may be reproduced, stored in a retrieval system, or transmitted in any form or by any means - electronic or mechanical, photocopy, recording, or any other - except for brief quotations in printed reviews, without the prior permission of the publisher. Although the author(s) and publisher have made every effort to ensure the accuracy and completeness of information contained in this book, we assume no responsibility for errors, inaccuracies, omissions, or any inconsistency herein.

*To everyone looking for
their special someone*

I always wished love was easy.

I wished I could just wake up one day, look in the mirror and say to myself,

"I'm ready to find the one," and then she just appears.

You know in those typical romance movies; where a guy walks down the street then sees the girl of his dreams as he peaks into a coffee shop for cappuccino? That was exactly what I thought I wanted. A coffee shop girl. A girl that I can find without having to look far and wide, like a prince in a love story, a girl that will make all my dreams come true, a girl that I could call my own…

A girl that would make me the happiest girl in the world.

Chapter One

Marissa Evans was so freaking beautiful. The kind of beauty that you only read in historical romance novels, the kind of beauty that allowed one to be a femme fatale to men in movies. That kind of beauty. That effortless beauty and grace that was so rare, Marissa had that.

The last thing on my mind when starting my sophomore year of high school was actually liking someone, like *really liking* someone. I steal a glance at her and my heart flutters at how beautiful her profile is.

Will she notice me? And if she does, will she also feel the same way?

As if hearing me, she turned her head and looked me square in the face. Our eyes met and I held my breath. All this must have happed in like 5 seconds flat but to me, it felt like a full twenty minutes. She looked at me a total of 4 seconds.

I fancied that the left side of her lips rose a little, that a ghost of a smile was formed, but I shook my head.

Don't let your imaginations run wild, kiddo.

I chuckled lightly to myself and went to my locker before heading to my first class. It was a C day at school so Orchestra was first.

I walked in class and went straight to the far left of the room. Sitting by the cello section on the first day was the best option for me. It was great spot to be seen enough but not too much where the conductor would call on me to read a portion of the class syllabus.

Another 5 minutes left on the clock till the start of class and of course Marissa, my crush, walks in. Violin case strapped to her back and everything about her so elegant.

We never played on the first day but it was nice to see her preparation. A bit of a turn on for me, honestly. She was just so proper and effortlessly girly.

I got out of my daze when I heard the classroom door fling open again.

"Kate! Welcome back," Cynthia shouted, followed by a high squeal. That was Cynthia, always squealing.

I looked over to Marissa and saw that she glanced towards our direction.

"What's up, Cynthia! How was your summer?" I asked, hugging her just as tight.

"Can't complain," she replied while plopping down on the seat,

"Helped out at this summer camp with my mom the whole time. There's so much we need to talk about. Come sit over here," she said patting the seat beside her.

Of course, she chose to sit one seat away from my crush but there was nothing I could do about it now. I got up and brushed my shirt down a few times to smoothen the wrinkles that formed from my slouch. I started to make my way toward Cynthia when Marissa and I locked eyes for a moment. I smiled her way, as to not be awkward because we had been having some pretty deep eye contact. She smiled back and then my dreams finally came true, she spoke to me.

Marissa spoke to me.

"Hey," she said with a slight smirk on her face. I didn't reply immediately, I felt like I was in a trance. Was this really happening? Did Marissa Evans just speak to me? I took a brief and anxious look around the classroom to make sure it was me she was talking to, stopping me in my tracks.

"Oh h-hey," I said. My nerves really got the best of me at that moment. I was always something of a charmer; smooth with words but at that moment, words eluded me.

"What's your name?" she asked.

But before I could answer, Mrs. Chen was already doing roll calls. I took my seat. The class silenced as Mrs. Chen went through the names. She gave us the course guidelines and told us all she expected of us. I couldn't stop looking at Marissa, her beautiful dark brown hair shown with gold flecks in it. Her skin was so smooth and she looked so willowy.

Vulnerable, beautiful.

A part of me just knew that she didn't know just how lovely she was because she was always polite. Everybody I have met always talks about her almost Victorian-like mannerisms. She had a natural-born etiquette.

When Mrs. Chen was done, she said that her class was an interactive one. She gave us permission to talk, lay our heads on our stands, or read our books during the rest of class time. Of course, all we wanted to do was talk.

"Hey again. Your name is..." Marissa said suddenly.

"Kate" I said, "Well, my name is Katherine but all my friends call me Kate. Katherine is fine too, y'know. I've just always been called Kate. I'll answer to anything really." Realizing that I was rambling like a lunatic, I paused and looked at the ground to calm myself. "What's your name though?"

"Okay, Kate" She lightly chuckled. "My name is Marissa, and please, stop being so shy. I have seen the way you talk to your friends."

"Hmm, you have? And um… I kind of already know your name."

Immediately the words left my mouth, I regretted it.

Way to go, sleek. Now you totally sound like you were stalking her.

I was about to explain that I wasn't a stalker, but her next words stopped me.

"And I kind of already knew your name was Kate Greenwood."

"Wow," I said, unable to mask my amazement.

I coughed a bit and said,

"I noticed your…" I pointed to her Violin case. "We never play on the first day but it's nice to see your preparation. Do you play very well?"

"Yes, you? And do you play others?"

"Quite, and I do play others. I play guitar, piano, saxophone, and a little drums as well."

"There's a piano in here…" She glanced over to the piano.

"Mhmmm" I nodded and smiled.

"So…"

"Yes, I'll play for you some time. Just not today."

"Y'all are so cute" Cynthia interrupted, startling me.

"What are you girls talking about? Wait, my bad. I'm Cynthia, what's your name?" she looked at Marissa who was a bit stunned but with a small smile tugging at her lips.

I could understand her feeling. Cynthia could be a bit too much sometimes.

"Marissa. Marissa Evans."

"Okay cool. You're very pretty," Cynthia said.

And I couldn't agree with Cynthia more. Of course, I couldn't say this out loud because I didn't want anyone to get the wrong idea or the right one, I guess.

The bell rang for us to head to our second classes. I figured this was my last chance to talk to Marissa until tomorrow's orchestra class so I tried to think of some impactful last words.

"Well, may your chi guide you today."

Nice one, weirdo.

I mentally face palmed myself and she replied, "that's a new one… I like it," and smiled at me before she sauntered away. My eyes followed her till I couldn't see her anymore.

My other friend, Nat, approached me and tapped me lightly on the shoulder, causing me to get out my trance and said, "Go for it, Kate."

"What do you mean? I have no idea" I asked, knowing what she meant but not wanting to admit it to myself.

"I think you do but it's okay. What's your next class?" she asked with a mock innocent expression that made me laugh.

"English, I think," I quickly shuffled through my backpack to find my class schedule, "Yep, I was right. English."

"Wow Same. Let's go," Nat said and waited for me to gather my things.

***

Throughout the whole day at school I couldn't stop thinking about my first encounter with Marissa. I wondered if she thought about me too. And if she did, what she thought about me and what could become of the entire situation.

At the end of the day I stood outside and waited for my dad to pick me up.

I waved to him as I saw his car approach and when I entered, I continued my day dream session about Marissa the whole way home.

"Awfully quiet back there," my dad said suddenly, startling me.

"Yea, I'm just tired."

"Don't say yea to me. It's yes or yes sir," he said curtly and I knew to prepare myself for a long lecture ahead that I've heard too many times. I rolled my eyes and waited.

"Back when I was in college..." I mentally groaned.

Not again.

"I went to class one day and my teacher, Ms. Guthrie, called on me and asked a question. I replied back and said yea and you know what she did?"

"No sir, no clue," I said automatically although I had heard the story a million times or more.

"She gave me such a scathing look and called me a mannerlessly spoiled brat. I can still remember it to this day. She said, "Mr. Greenwood, in this classroom you say yes."

I turned up the volume of my headphones till it drowned out his voice.

The smell of rotisserie chicken and soft music greeted me when I walked into the house. My mother was in the kitchen.

"Kate! How was the first day?" I could tell she was excited to have some type of mother-daughter sit down talk session about my first day of school but I just wasn't in the mood. I'm sure she just wanted to know if things went wrong and how to blame me for them going wrong.

The truth was that, I just don't vibe with my parents. If my parents weren't my parents, there is a very high possibility that I wouldn't like them.

"My day was fine. I'm just really tired," I said, feigning a yawn as I dragged my feet up to my room.

I shut the door and laid on my bed. I was lost in thoughts.

I had my first real crush on a girl and couldn't tell anyone about it. Of course, I've liked other girls in the past but none of them made my heart move like Marissa. I just met her and already knew this was something special. I always knew that I was drawn to girls and I've tried so hard to fight it.

I knew when I was six and had a little crush on Sophie Blake, my old grade school mate.

As I got older, I thought it would fade and I tried to force myself to like guys. But it just wasn't happening. I just found myself drawn to the contours of a woman's body.

And I knew I could never tell anyone, at least. I come from a religious home; too freaking fake and religious.

My mom would be more concerned about the embarrassment my *lifestyle* would cause her than the actual impact it had on me.

I shook my head at the thoughts. For now, it would just be my little secret.

Chapter Two

For the rest of the week, my heart pounded each time I walked into the orchestra class. Somehow, Marissa always beat me there first and would a save a seat for me. The first time she did it, I felt my heart melt but pretty soon, it became a regular occurrence.

Cynthia and Nat also joined us and after a while, we all became pretty close. Marissa was so much more fun and livelier and more mischievous than I ever envisioned and I loved the fact that I learned something new about her every day.

We get in trouble with Mrs. Chen for our noisemaking, but we always had a good time regardless.

"Oh my gosh!" Cynthia exclaimed, one day "we need to totally talk about this. I know y'all saw Kasey and Alexis getting close in the cafeteria this morning, right?"

"Oh what… really?" Nat asked, bug eyed

"Yea. They're basically a whole couple now I think."

"They probably are though, seems like everyone is getting together nowadays," Nat glanced at Marissa and I and stifled a cough.

"This is a small school, with majority women, so we're bound to see it a lot more. I support it though," Marissa said, blank faced.

I looked over at Marissa and thought to myself.

Does she support because she is gay or because she just supports it?

I didn't want to ask directly but I was dying to know

"Mhm, that's true," I said in response to Marissa's statement.

"I swore you were gay, to be honest," Cynthia chuckled and looked at me dead in the eyes, my heart skipped and I felt the breath leave my body but I maintained a blank face.

"Oh me? C'mon girl. Please," I said noncommittally.

I felt weird because what if Marissa was into girls? But I'd rather maintain a straight reputation until I am sure of my own feelings. Being different came with a lot of negativity and for now, I was comfortable being in my closet. It was better that way.

"Kasey is a hoe though. She's gotten with almost every girl at this school. She's even tried to turn me out but it's a big no for me," Nat said, making us all giggle.

***

I stood up from my bed to go get a glass of milk. On my way back up, I heard the loud ding of the notification bell on my phone. I checked and apparently, Kasey had sent me a direct message.

My heart started to beat fast and I was confused. Why would Kasey be texting me at this time?

I sat on my bed for a moment and thought what could Kasey possibly want from me? Nat did say that she was known for trying to turn girls out.

I opened the message and it read, " Hey" with two heart eye emojis. I thought why not and proceeded to message back, "Hey, what's up?"

"You know who this is?" she replied.

"Sure, Kasey," I sent.

"Are you surprised?. Lol," she returned.

"Um... a bit. Why are you texting though?"

"I think you know, Kate," she replied making my heart start to hammer.

"I don't. You tell me."

"Well, I find you super, super cute, Kate…"

"I'm grateful, Kasey. You're pretty hot too."

"Wanna meet up somewhere in school tomorrow so we could talk better?"

"Okay cool," I replied. I sent her my number and she texted me saying I should store her number.

I liked Marissa but I was so excited. Kasey was beautiful. She had that brown-eyed brown-haired thing going on for her and it worked fine. I had never been with any woman in my life and it was my greatest fantasy. I was thinking about possible things I could do with Kasey and I found that I was getting slightly aroused.

All night long, I stayed up thinking about the whole situation. I just wondered what we would talk about or do.

Will she try and kiss me? Will I respond? Do I want it? Can I resist that body of hers? What would Marissa think?

As I thought about Marissa, I felt a bit bad for thinking about Kasey and I argued that I did nothing wrong. After all, Marissa and I are nothing.

Tomorrow was going to be a dramatic day. It's best I get some sleep right now, I thought to myself even as I dozed off.

The next day finally came and I all but ran into the school when I was dropped off. I had come early just so that I could stay at the cafeteria to hang out with my friends. The cafeteria is that place where students stay to pass the time before lectures began.

But as I stepped in, what I saw made me retrace my steps. I saw Marissa and Kasey in a tight embrace and when they separated, Kasey ran her hand through Marissa's braids.

What the f?

Chapter Three

When the final bell rang to dismiss orchestra class, I pulled Marissa to the side, "Hey, can I talk to you for a second?" I asked. I didn't know how I managed to stay sane all through the day, but I did. The image of Marissa and Kasey tormented me though. I told myself that I was overreacting but I couldn't help it.

"Sure, okay," she replied, looking a bit startled.

"So, um… I…I saw you earlier."

"What do you mean?" she asked, wide-eyed.

"I saw you in the cafeteria with Kasey. What's up with that? I know it's not my business but I-"

Marissa cut me off, giggling sweetly as she said, "we were just talking,"

"Do you talk to her? Like, do you like her? Because what I saw was way more than talking. I saw her give you a big hug and I didn't even know… even know that…that," I didn't know where my jealousy was stemming from.

"You're asking if I'm gay right?" Marissa chuckled, her eyes twinkling.

"I guess so, yea," I said with a sigh, unable to hide my curiosity (and hope) anymore.

"That's for me to know and for you to find out. And about Kasey, we do talk. She got my number and texted me one time and we just hit it off."

"That's crazy," I said, pausing to collect my thoughts, "well fine. Just be careful, I guess."

Why do I feel like crying all of a sudden? Urgh.

"And why is that? It's nothing serious, we're just texting," Marissa asked, a look of doubt on her face.

"Fine," I sighed, "I'm just going to be honest. Can I trust you, Marissa?"

"Of course, you can," she said, and stepped closer to me.

Looking at her, I decided to put all my cards on the table.

"I got jealous. I was jealous that she was making you smile like that. I was jealous that she touched your hair. Hell, I was jealous that she hugged you! I don't know why but I was jealous. I don't usually feel that way and it feels so weird and oh my goodness, I am so rambling now so I guess I will just shut the fuck up and scram away."

Marissa just stared while I talked and as I turned to leave, she held me back and said "that is by far the cutest thing anybody has ever said to me before."

"How is that even possible?" I asked in disbelief. She was so damn cute. It should be a regular thing.

"Kate, just take what I say," she said, her eyes twinkling prettily, "I'm actually happy you feel that way because honestly, I was thinking you and Cynthia had something and I was kind of envious that she had you all to herself.. But that was way before I found out you guys were just good friends."

"Really?" I asked yet again in absolute disbelief and at her nod, I felt something move in me. I wanted to have Marissa, to have her be mine.

"Well, yeah… Really. I'm happy my thoughts were wrong though," she said. Playfully nudging me and making me giggle.

I looked up at the clock. "Well, we both need to head to lunch now but um… can I get your contact? So that I'd like text you and stuff?

"Um… I thought you'd never ask," grinning, she called off her digits and told me her handles on social media (as if I didn't know them already.)

We both paused and just looked at each other before shyly smiling and heading to the cafeteria

***

Marissa and I became almost inseparable and the next two months, we basically talked every night. We also met up at school in the morning, and again after school just to talk. We bonded so much, she felt like a real part of me. I had never really been comfortable around anyone as I was with her. She made me absolutely happy and that was something alien to me. Like a text from her could light up my entre day. She wasn't much of a talker naturally but with me, she went off. She always had me in tears with laughter by the end of each day and it was surprising that she was that witty. Like, her sense of humor was phenomenal. She was sarcastic and so sassy when she wanted to be.

We also had so much in common; from the types of food we liked to art and music we listened to. I wouldn't have traded her for anything in the world and I loved how all my friends just accepted us. I still had a crush on her. In fact, it was growing bigger than a crush but I had to keep my cool so as not to creep her out.

We still hadn't talked about her sexuality since that time and I didn't want to jinx anything. I didn't want to scare her either.

There were nights where my parents would come into my room to talk and I was glad that I had Marissa because they always looked for a way to make me feel stupid and unserious with my life. They were always so condescending.

"Every day you get one step closer to graduating. You don't even act like someone that is almost done with high school. I don't know what it is but whatever it is, I do hope you have you been looking at colleges?" My dad would ask with that arrogant look on his face. That look that made me want to spit at his feet.

"Yes, I have," I'd reply like the obedient drone that I am. My replies never varied.

My mother would come in and give her two cents, "I don't care where you go, just make sure it's an HBCU. No daughter of mine would settle for less. You don't do much as it is so the least you could do is go to a good college. Let people see that *my* daughter is getting the best of the best."

"And after that, you have to start looking for jobs. You could even start now. Don't be like your older brother and wait till the last minute to handle your business. He is a miscreant and sometimes I ask where I went wrong with that boy. But not to worry, we're relying on you, Katherine," my dad would add in.

They repeated themselves like a broken record almost every night but I pretty soon figured that they didn't really care about my happiness or education. They cared more about fanning the flames of their ego.

They would leave my room with their nose in the air, proud of themselves like they should win the award for best parents.

The moment they'd leave, I'd go back to texting the one soul that always made me happy.

***

"Katherine, what is this?" my mother thundered as she lifted up a pair of red basketball shorts from my drawer. She held it between the tips of her fingers like it was contaminated and I tried my possible best to keep my expression calm.

In actuality, I was panicking *madly*.

She wasn't supposed to see them. How could I be so dumb and forget to bury them deeper in the exact spot I always do.

"Uh those must be James's," I said, coming up with the lie on that spot.

"We did laundry together yesterday," I continued. I was super fluent at lying to my parents. It wasn't that I enjoyed lying, it's just that nothing I ever do is good enough. Especially to my mother.

Roseline Greenwood was that woman that wanted me to be everything she wasn't growing up. She didn't come from a well to do family and only got into the limelight when she married my father.

She always tried to project all her girlish, teenage fantasies on me and honestly, it was irritating and unsettling but I don't have a choice than to take it.

"Mhmm okay. I'll put them in his room then, she said, turning to leave.

She stopped again and looked around at me, saying, "you better not be lying to me either. It's not becoming of a young lady to wear men's clothing." And with that, she was out of the door.

Mother could never stand me wearing shorts or jerseys "like a man." If it didn't have bows or ribbons or weird bright colors or something that popstars wore, it wasn't good enough for my mom.

It was always as if she wanted me to be a barbie, something that was so alien to my nature.

When my mom left, I stood up and shut my door properly, locking it.

I tucked myself into the bed and texted Marissa to see if she was still awake. I waited for about 15 minutes before I started drifting off. In my semi-conscious state, I felt a hard vibration from my phone.

It was a text from her.

"I think we should do it tomorrow after school," She sent.

I immediately came awake like I was electrocuted and replied, "Do what?"

"That's for you to find out. I like it when I give you a mystery to crack open, plus I want you to look forward to something."

"you are such a tease," I replied, loving every second of it.

The more I spent time with Marissa, the more I wanted her. I wanted to give her pleasure like never before and I loved the fact that we tease each other.

"Tomorrow after school then…."

I felt a little anxious and super excited as I replied, "hmm, okay, you witch. Looking forward to this *mystery*. Btw, I said mystery in Scooby-Doo's voice."

She replied with a laughter and I smiled as I drifted up into a sleep filled with my actual dream girl; filled with Marissa.

Chapter Four

At school the next day I walked around with a little extra swag in my step. Literature was my last class for the day and it was all I could do to not check the class clock every five minutes. Just as I was about to roll my eyes for the millionth time, the bell rang.

As soon as the bell rung, I pulled out my phone from my backpack and texted Marissa to know where she was. I waited for a couple of minutes but got no reply. That was pretty strange, considering how quickly she texts back. I guessed she was busy and decided to go wait at my locker. I headed to my locker along with my friend Alexis. She was a bit of a talker so, her endless stream of conversation kept my head clear.

"I cannot wait for the holidays, girl. My birthday coming up and it is going to be sick! I don't know if I want to throw a huge party or something though. What do you think?" Alexis asked me.

Knowing who Alexis was, I'm quite sure that she will throw a huge party. That's just how the girl is.

"Not sure. Were you thinking of a whole ass event or just something small for family only?" I asked, as we approached our lockers knowing what the end result would be.

"Hmm, maybe something small but I don't know. It depends on my mood.," Alexis's words started to fade as soon as we turned the corner to our lockers. Marissa was standing right beside mine, waiting for me. I realized that I could get used to seeing her beautiful, brown face any day and any time.

"Whatever you decide, I'm here for you. I'll text you later," I quickly said to end the conversation with Alexis, "Fancy seeing you here, Mari."

"I saw your text but thought it would be better if I just met you here. Thought I'd surprise you for once," She looked me up and down, smiling.

I smirked and opened my locker, "I like that, I could get used to this kind of surprise. How were your classes today? Sucks we didn't have orchestra today."

"They weren't bad, not at all. So where should we go?" she asked.

I tossed my backpack on to the floor and opened my locker to put my backpack inside.

"Since school just ended, we should probably give it a minute so that we can find a private place. We can just walk around in the meantime. I told my parents that I have to stay a little longer at school for a club meeting. You?"

"Yea. This morning I said the same."

"I can't wait for us to be old enough to do whatever we want to do without permission from anybody!"

We first walked around the locker room and the cafeteria to socialize with our friends. After about twenty minutes we gave each other a look. A look that said more than actual words can. A look that made my blood boil and my heart race. The locker rooms, hallways, and main stair cases were clear as almost everyone had gone home. We walked out the cafeteria together and headed towards the orchestra practice rooms. They were always empty after school and were private enough for students to loiter around intimately.

"Ladies, coming in to do some practicing?" Mrs. Chen greeted us at the door cheerfully. It was so unexpected that I almost dropped my cell phone. I didn't expect anyone to be there.

"Not today" we both chuckled and continued to walk on past the practice rooms.

Marissa and I gave each other a look and burst into laughter. We knew how close that was.

"What now?" Marissa asked.

"We're right by the gym."

"You know the basketball team is probably in there by now."

"Hmmn, the bathroom! What about the bathroom? Let's just go in and see."

"I'm cool with that," she replied, a hint of doubt crossing her face.

I looked at her and told her that if she wasn't comfortable, she could leave. It wasn't a do or die affair. But she assured me that she was alright, just a tad nervous.

"Wait here," I said and walked ahead to see if the coast was clear. It was. I did a light fist bump in the air and headed back out to usher her in.

"Hey Mari, guess what?" I said.

"What?" Julia replied.

"What the fuck!" I squealed, almost banging my head on the wall in fright.

Julia was one of our close mutual friends but what in the world was she doing in here?! What if I hadn't spoken? Is that how she would have caught us in the act? I looked at Marissa and she shrugged back at me. First Mrs. Chen and now this? It felt like nature was just giving us reasons to not be together.

I chuckled nervously, "Nothing. What's up Julia? What are you doing here?"

"I was just hanging with the basketball team for a bit but it got boring. Then I decided to come powder my nose."

She looked at Marissa, then me then Marissa again before saying,

"Did y'all see if any practice rooms were open? I want to hear you play piano, Kate. You promised me a song one day."

I looked at Marissa then back at Julia, "that would have to wait, girl. I'm somewhat busy now and besides, Mrs. Chen is on her way out."

Julia smiled at Marissa, "aaahhh, busy huh?" she asked with a smug look on her face.

"Oh wow. I knew it!" Julia squealed after a few seconds. She had put two and two together.

"This explains so much. Have y'all been a couple this whole time?"

Mari and I looked at her very innocently, like we didn't know what she was talking about.

"Wow y'all. That's great. Even if you don't say anything, I can see the attraction from a mile away. You both have my full support on this. Go ahead, get your freak on," she flapped both her hands in a forward motion at us and then giving an exaggerated wink, she sauntered away from the bathroom.

Marissa finally followed me into the restroom and I suddenly felt like someone blocked my oxygen. I didn't know what to do. This was the moment I'd been waiting for, for the longest time and now it was here, I had no idea what to do.

"So…" Marissa said in a shaky voice and when I looked at her, I saw she was blushing. She looked so beautiful. Her brown skin shone like it was carved out of the finest wood and oiled.

My fears disappeared as I looked at her because I knew more than ever that I wanted her all to myself. Right then, kissing her was the only thing in my head.

I slowly walked close to her, going closer till I backed her against the wall.

With my face inches apart from hers, I asked quietly, "what's on your mind?"

Marissa looked as though she was having second thoughts about this moment but something on my face must have cleared her doubts.

"I don't know," she said in a small voice, "Do you think we're rushing this?"

"Not at all. Marissa, I've never been surer about anyone or anything in my life."

She leaned in towards me with her eyes closed and that was how we had our first kiss. Our lips met halfway and it was indeed sensational.

It was better than anything I had ever imagined. Her lips were so soft and warm underneath mine I thought I was going to bruise her at first but after a while, I got so consumed by the taste of hers.

While we kissed, I thought to myself, *I'm really here. We're really doing this,* and I backed away from her.

"What's wrong, Kate?" she asked when she noticed how heavy I was breathing. But I couldn't answer her. I felt so happy yet scared at the same time. How could I tell her that she was evoking feelings in me I never even knew I had? I ran out of the bathroom, barely seeing anyone in my way. I didn't even notice Julia on my way. I continued down the hallway only stopping when I got to my locker and that was only because Marissa was calling me.

"What's going on?" she said curtly, slightly out of breath, "I thought this is what we wanted, what you wanted."

I felt terrible for making her feel that way, for hurting her feelings.

"It is," I replied, "I promise it is. Hell, it is more than I even anticipated. But I-"

"You what?" she snapped.

"I like you a lot, Marisa, so much. So much that it hurts sometimes. And I just wanna know, do you like me too?"

"Yes, of course. You know this."

"So why does this all feel so wrong? Like why do I have to have my first kiss with my favorite woman in a freaking bathroom stall? I know I like you and want to be with you but I'm scared. I want to be able to not have to wait until after school to kiss who I want. I want to hold you and show you off without having to hide it. All these crazy thoughts ran through my head when our lips touched. I like you so much more than I even anticipated."

"Oh my goodness… I don't know what to say, Kate. I don't even know… I thought *I* was the only person that went through that. I didn't know you felt that way too."

I smiled because I couldn't believe she felt that way and for some reason, I felt so much better. "This is just crazy. Who knew being different came with all this," I said.

She started to smile, "Just stop being gay then."

I looked up at Marissa and we both broke out into laughter,

"Yeah right, and lose you?" I said. I pulled her close and gave her a big hug. Maybe one day, I will be bold enough to kiss her again in an open setting.

As she walked away, I took in her soft brown skin, her long braids that went all the way to her back and I shook my head in amazement; what a girl.

Chapter Five

"I wish we could hang out outside of school," Marissa said via text, "you should come over some time."

"I would love to. I just don't know how my parents would react. I don't go out that much, besides to school events and if my parents hear that I am going to see a girl… ahhhh!!"

"How about tonight? I want to see you," she said in that cute, whiny voice that I could barely resist.

"Oh really?"

"Yes. That first kiss just wasn't enough. I want more. I love the way you take charge, Kate. I want more."

Every two weeks, my parents went on Friday dinner dates to a classy restaurant at the other end of the town.

Tonight was one of those nights so, I thought to myself, why not? And my brother wasn't home. Why not just do it?

"Okay. My parents are heading out soon. I'll come over when they leave," I said with excitement.

***

At exactly 6:30pm I heard the sound of mother's heels hit the kitchen floor, followed by the hard clump sound of my dad's dress shoes. Those sounds never failed to give me reassurance of peaceful night but tonight was different. Tonight, I felt like a spy that was about to embark on a dangerous mission.

They gave me the rules of the house as usual even though they've said them to me every week for the past five years, then headed out to the car. I waited by the window to make sure they were gone. After they left, I quickly headed to my drawer and reached down to the bottom to pull out my favorite jeans and a t-shirt that I kept hidden from my parents. All the clothes I actually liked, I kept shoved at the bottom of drawer or back of my closet. Seeing how my mother reacted to the basketball shorts caused me to take extra precautions when buying clothes in secret.

I put on my clothes and packed an extra bag of "feminine" clothes, in case my parents made it home before me and I needed to change before entering the house. There were some clothes that my mother approved of. She liked frilly things, like that would make me the barbie she wants me to be so bad.

I sent a text to Marissa that I was on my way and she replied with a cute, kissy emoji. I waited for a few minutes, making sure my parents were gone for good.

Then, I grabbed my bag, keys and phone before I headed to the car. I made it to Marissa's in a few minutes time and I swear, I had one of the best evenings I ever had with her.

"Isn't this a little awkward for you?" I whispered to Marissa, after greeting her mom in the kitchen.

Mrs. Evans was so nice and she actually squeezed my cheeks and called me a "cutie." She was really warm and motherly, something my mother was the exact opposite of.

"Her daughter is just hanging out with another girl. That's all she sees. There is no reason for her to think otherwise," Marissa said reassuringly, flashing me her beautiful smile.

We started the night by seeing a movie and talking. I knew how easy it was talking to Marissa but the reality was staggering again. She was such a delight.

I did three pats on the bed in the spot next to me after the first movie finished and said, "Scooch closer to me."

She did, of course, saying, "I thought you'd never ask."

I put my arm around her and she curled up into a little ball next to me, placing her head on my chest and right arm across my stomach. It felt so natural and I couldn't help but peck her forehead at intervals.

"You think we're ready?" she asked in a small voice.

I took a deep breath and responded, "I don't know much about this, honestly, but I do know that I want to be with you more than everyone I have ever crushed on."

"Even more than Meagan Good?" she asked jokingly because she knew how crazy I was about the actress, Meagan Good.

"Meagan Good is nothing compared to you, Mari."

"Oh Kate…" she said in that breathless whisper that drove me crazy.

She glanced up at me then put her head back down on my chest. I saw the lust in her eyes.

I placed my left hand under her chin and brought her lips up to meet mine. We kissed softly until it felt like we were merging into one person. I felt her right hand move from around my torso uncertainly. Like she didn't know if she should do whatever it was she had in mind. I squeezed her hand to encourage her and she started fondling and caressing my breasts through my top. She lifted my shirt and headed towards my bra and started to fondle my already hard nipples. She wanted to put her hand inside my cloth to touch the raw skin but grabbed her hand before it reached the bottom of my cloth.

"I want you first, I want to please you." I said, "Let me try."

I raised her tank top up to her neck and I gasped. She was close to perfect. Her skin was so brown and beautiful and her breasts were a sight to behold with their chocolate areolas and even darker nipples. I couldn't help it, I bent my head downward and flicked a tongue against one nipple. She sighed softly and ached her back farther up into my mouth.

"Okay wow. You are really the most gorgeous girl in this world," I lightly chuckled while looking down at her underwear.

She looked down and laughed with me, "C'mon. babe… please."

I knew what she wanted and closed my mouth over her erect nipple. I had to place my hand over her mouth to stop her from moaning so nicely but damn, she tasted good. I alternated between both breasts. Suckling on one and fondling the other before vice versa.

I crawled up to her and kissed her lips some more, not believing I just did that.

"You're really okay with all this?" I asked.

"Yes, I promise," she said, her eyes glazed with passion, "now, your turn."

From that moment on we were able to connect on a level that neither of us had experienced before. Although it wasn't the best, since we both had no prior experience, we were both there physically and mentally. Most importantly, we were both happy and wanted to do this. Once we finished, or done doing what we thought was close enough to actually "doing it," we just laid there and looked each other's naked torso, moving our hands across each other's body in admiration. I couldn't believe that she was all mine.

Thoughts of my parents crept into my mind, but I shoved them way. I don't need them crowding my blessing. I knew I'd probably be a little late but I always had a good lie to say and I hoped they wouldn't be too tough on me.

We both turned towards the tv and continued to watch the movie we left playing. The clock hit around nine and I tapped Marissa on the shoulder, "I think I should go now," I said in disbelief. I didn't know that time had moved that fast.

Urgh, time flies when you are having fun.

"You sure?"

"Yea. I need to beat my parents' home. I'll talk to you later, babe. But I really have to leave," I said dressing up very quickly. I had to get home before my parents!

Marissa walked me to the door and kissed me good bye.

I pulled off in my car, glancing back at her until she disappeared from my sight. I made it to the highway and was about five minutes away from home when I heard my phone vibrate. I glanced at the caller ID and it was my mother.

Oh shit!

Chapter Six

"Where are you?" my mother snapped the moment I picked up. She didn't even answer my greeting.

"Umm I'm out just grabbing some food, I-" I said.

"It's late. Come home now!" she yelled, hanging up the phone.

I arrived home and my parents were in the kitchen waiting for me. They are almost always mad at me for something so I already knew the drill. I walked up to my mother and handed her my phone without a word.

"Exactly. You already know how this goes," she said smugly.

"You just got a license, but that doesn't mean you should be driving anywhere at any time," my dad said.

"Isn't that the point of a license though?" I replied sarcastically before I could hold my tongue.

Oh boy.

"Stop being disrespectful to us and go to your room," he said, his right eye twitching and his fist balled up.

I went to my room and texted Marissa from my laptop, "hey, they're at it again. Don't text or call me for the rest of the night. I'll see you at school."

I finished up my homework just barely because my thoughts were filled with Marissa. It was all about her for me. After my assignment, I headed off to bed with the biggest smile on my face. The trouble with my parents didn't even bother me as much as it would have because I got to be with Marissa. And even if it was for a little while, outside of school, it was worth it.

I couldn't sleep so I stayed up most of the night recalling our time together.

Around 3am I heard my phone start to ring from my parents' room. I really hoped it wasn't Marissa. Neither of my parents came to me or anything which was a good sign, or not. It only rang once and I made sure to change Marissa's name in my phone before walking into the house. Everything should be fine…or so I imagined. If I had known how drastically my life would change, I might have had a heart attack.

***

The next morning my mother came to into my room asking me for the password to my phone. I gave it to her without thinking because I was super sleepy and she left my room. In the time she had my phone she must've went through everything; my messages, photos, and all of my social media but I doubt she'd find anything because I deleted most of the very implicating texts the night before in my car when she called.

Loud and hard footsteps came towards my room not so long after my mother had left my room and I knew that shit was about to hit the fan. She pushed open my door and gave me a scalding look. She was madder than I had ever seen her before.

"What the hell is this? Explain this to me!" she yelled, with a picture of Marissa and I up on my phone. The picture was a bit suggestive but not quite. Marissa and I were in a side embrace and she was captured giving me a peck on my cheek.

I quickly sat upright on my bed. "It's just my friend," I said, calmly. Showing any sign of nervousness will make my mom go berserk. I know her too well.

"I don't like this at all. Nice girls shouldn't take these kinds of photos."

She deleted the picture and then went to my messages. "And what kind of friend do you message like this? I don't message my friends like this."

My heart almost beat out of my chest, I was so scared. "Mom, they're just slangs, I promise."

She looked at me for a long moment and threw my phone at me,

"Is this the food you went to get, huh? Hanging out with some little bitch from your school."

Tears started to form in my eyes. "Don't ever call her that, mom. She did nothing. She's just a friend," I said.

I knew that the crying would soften her. My mom loved to feel in charge and I was just giving her what she wanted. I wanted to come out there and then, but I wasn't ready. I just had my first make out session with another girl yesterday. That in its own was even too much for me to handle, talk more of telling my mom that I'm gay. That will have to wait till Marissa and I solidify what we have.

She looked at me as though my words were a challenge to her dominance in the room. "I want you out of my house if you will keep behaving like this and keeping useless friends. Just wait till I tell your father when he gets home," she started to smile, a devilish look, before continuing her loud rant.

My brother, James, ran out of his room, "What is going on in here?"

"Go back to your room James!" my mother replied, "It's none of your business."

"My sister is in here crying. It is my business. What's wrong, Kate?" he looked at me in shock that my mother was behaving this way.

I looked up at him, "she saw a picture I took with my classmate and now..." I said very low, almost like a whisper

"So.. what's the problem?" He looked confused, "That's why you're upset with her? What kind of mother are you?"

My mom threw the phone at him and he looked more perplexed than ever. I knew that I had to tell my brother the truth, very soon. I needed to know how he'd react.

Glancing at my mother, I was glad that she bought the story that Mari was *just a friend*.

In the past seventeen years of my life, I had never been as scared as I was right there and then. I just couldn't come out now, no! I just accepted this part of myself. My mother kept yelling and yelling. She kept going on and on about how irresponsible I was becoming and how much of bad influences my friends were.

I said nothing. I just bowed my head and allowed her say all she had to. It's better for her to think what she was thinking than know the truth.

My mother called together a family meeting that night when my dad got home which I knew would not end well.

It started with my mother telling everyone what she saw on my phone; the picture of Marissa and I.

"I want you all take a good look at what our daughter," She looked my father, "and your beloved sister," she glanced at James, "has been up to."

Nothing was inappropriate but it was clear that my father would support her. They always supported each other in making our lives miserable.

After my mother finished speaking, James grabbed my hand under the table and shook it. This was our secret sign of saying, "I'm here with you," during times like this when our parents would start to belittle us.

My dad started to chime in, "We pay so much for you to attend that school and this what you do? Make silly friends."

James grabbed my hand tighter and defended me, "but you don't even know this girl! You just saw a random picture and you're judging? What's wrong with a girl giving her friend a hug and a peck? At least it's a good thing she can get hugs somewhere because she sure as hell ain't getting any in this house." He stared at my mother waiting for a comeback, his muscles flexing underneath his peach colored muscle tee but she just looked at me.

She nudged my father, "You're going to let your son talk to me that way?" she asked him but my father just remained silent. I knew that they were both a bit scared of James. I don't know what he did to them, but it was pretty effective.

We all stayed quiet for a few more minutes, both my parents looking at me so I figured that everyone had calmed down a bit. I started to talk, "I'm sorry for the picture, mom. But I didn't know that there was anything wrong that picture. That was why I gave you my phone, mom. With no hesitation."

My dad banged his hands on the table, got up, and walked over to me. He got very close to me, bringing his face just two inches away from mine,

"Just stop stressing your mom and I!"

I nodded my head, hiding the triumph I felt. Yes, they bought the story!!

My father continued, "As for you, son," he slid James chair out from under the table and stood in front of him, "don't you ever speak to your mother like that again or I'll kick you right out of here. As much as we've spent on the both of you and this is how you treat us?"

While my dad barked, I drifted off. I was way too happy that my relationship with Marissa was safe at least. I closed my eyes to drown out the sound of my father's voice, focusing only on Marissa's smile, her voice and that funny thing she did with her brows.

I went on to pray for Marissa and wished that her parents, if they find out about her or us, don't treat her like this because I know the day these ones will find out, all hell will break lose.

I heard my mother call my name but I ignored her until she and my dad called me simultaneously.

"Go up to your room, Katherine. We're done here," my father said. I could see that he was a tad bit surprised that I wasn't bawling as usual, like a baby.

I got up from the table and pushed my chair in turning to leave.

"One more thing!" my mother said. I looked over at her, my face expressionless, "you need to clean your face up but here's your phone. She slid it across the table to me.

"We love you but you need to make better decisions," she said.

All I wanted to do was talk to Marissa but I just couldn't. I kept my phone switched off for the rest of the day.

After I heard my parents go into their room, I gently stood up from my bed and snuck to the door. Very slowly, I cracked open my door and tiptoed to James's bedroom.

I did our special knock; a kind of knock that only James and I knew about.

I heard his lock turn and I stepped into his perpetually disorganized room.

"I figured you'd come, Rugrat," James said. Rugrat was the nickname he gave me when we were younger.

I knew that I had to do it now or never. James was literally the person I trusted the most in the world and if not him, then nobody else.

"Jamie, I'm gay."

Chapter Seven

"Jamie, I'm gay."

My heart was beating so fast and I felt like the ground should open so that it'd swallow me up. I love my brother so much. James and I have been each other's support system from the moment we could think because of the type of parents we have.

I looked at him and he looked at me for what seemed like twenty minutes but in actuality was about just 15 seconds.

I wasn't prepared for the next thing that came out of his mouth.

"Um… I kinda always knew, Rugrat. I think I've known since you were like eight years old or so but I was just waiting for you to tell me. Or rather, get comfortable enough to tell me."

"Wh...what?" I asked in disbelief. I couldn't believe it. How did he? What the…? What?!!

James chuckled and flung away a sweatshirt from a chair so I'd sit on it.

"I said that I knew you liked girls, Kate. Come on, you're my sister. And you know an insane number of guys have been crushing on you. I see the way you don't care. You *genuinely* didn't care. But I see the way you look at them girls, especially Vanessa. Remember Vanessa?"

I gasped.

Vanessa was one of the first girls I crushed on the moment I entered high school. She was three classes ahead of me (James's classmate) but to me, she was more beautiful than Aphrodite. In fact, she *was* Aphrodite.

"You knew? You knew about my feelings for Vanessa?" I asked my brother, my eyes tearing up because of the overwhelming love I felt for him at this moment.

"I knew, my baby girl. You're my sister. I know practically everything and I know that you steal my muscle tees and shorts sometimes," he said, smiling and pinching my nose as he said the last statement.

"So, you don't hate me? You don't find me disgusting?"

"What?" he asked looking as incredulous as ever, "find you disgusting because you like women? The fuck am I gonna do that for? How does your sexual preference affect who you are or what you do? Cmon girl. You know your bro is a real nigga."

"Oh Jamie," I said and flew into his arms, sobbing. I didn't know why I was sobbing, I guess it was because of the acceptance, *real* acceptance. He loved me for who I was and he knew. He knew all these years and not once did his attitude change towards me.

He held me till I couldn't sob anymore.

"Goddamn, Jamie… you don't even know what this means to me. It has been a burden to me. I- I am so scared. Mom and dad might literally kill me if they find out. Yo, they gonna whoop my ass and then kill me and then kill my corpse! Especially mom!"

"Well, they definitely ain't gonna find out from me that's for sure. And when they do, because you can't hide it forever, I got your back."

I hugged my brother again, feeling lighter than ever. He still loves me. Yes, Jamie still loves me. He means more to me that both my parents put together.

There and then, I told him about Marissa and we talked for a while. I told him about the kiss and he gave me a hi-five. I had to go sleep eventually because of school and I hugged him again and thanked him before I tiptoed back to my room.

When I got to my room, I silently danced around with joy. My brother's acceptance was one of the fears I'd always had and the fact that he even knew all these years just solidified my love for him which was already pretty solid.

At least, I had Jamie's blessings. Things will be better.

That night, I went to sleep with a very big smile on my face.

***

The first thing I did when I got to school that morning was find Marissa and tell her about everything that happened.

"My brother knew," I said, "he knew everything for years."

"Are you serious? And he didn't flip? He didn't do nothing?" she asked, her eyes growing round with disbelief. She knew how uptight my family was and hearing that James was okay with it was unbelievable to her. It still was to me myself.

"I love the fact that Jamie is okay with it, but I hate this feeling," I said with tears starting to form in my eyes, "I hate the fact that I can't bring you home. I hate that we have to hide to do everything. But what about you? If your parents asked or found out, please deny. Deny it all! I don't want you getting into any trouble because of me, especially if your folks are anything like mine."

"I would never deny how I feel about you," Marissa said as she started to cry as well, "I don't want us to ever feel or be alone if we get into this type of mess. Promise?"

"I promise," I said, choking back a fresh set of tears. I didn't know what I did to deserve such an angel but whatever brought her to me should keep her with me for a long time.

We hugged each other as tight as we could until the first bell rang. It was hard to let go.

The rest of the school day, Marissa and I would meet up in the bathroom every few hours to talk and kiss, of course.

I mostly talked about the fear I felt when my mother barged into my room. Even still remembering it made me shiver.

"I got you, babe. I got you," Marissa would say to me and then we'd hug and kiss a bit.

Our third time meeting up in the day, I just held her. I loved how soft and smooth her skin was. She looked like she was made out of actual caramel. So brown and beautiful; so soft and understanding. Her empathy was one of her most attractive qualities to me.

"Right now, it's just you and me here. Your parents aren't here. These are the moments we should take in and enjoy while we can," she said, her voice vibrating on my shoulder.

"I'm just overthinking. I'm scared to go home; I don't want to see my parents. I'm beginning to hate them," I said, starting to pace.

I pace when I'm agitated and the thought of going home sure agitated the hell out of me.

"Feel my heart beat, babe. It's just you and me here," Marissa said coming up to me and looking into my eyes. I looked at her and took a breath, realizing that the safest place for me is in her arms and out of my head.

Oh Mari, I'm so lucky to have you…

I went to school every day and tried to make it seem like Marissa and I were just friends. But the more I saw her, the more I liked her, the more I wanted her for me and me alone. All my close friends already knew about my sexuality by that time after they had a meeting to pry it out of me. I resented home each day because I was always greeted by some petty comment by my mom. One day, I actually wanted to retort and blast her back but James's eyes stopped me.

"Welcome home, sweetie," my mom would say, "Go sit down at the table, it's time to start your lesson."

She would sit down next to me and flip open her laptop. There would already be a video up on the screen. Each day was something different. These were ultra girly videos of snobby kids that got into highbrow universities like Yale or videos of girls just being extremely girly doing their makeup, dressing up in colorful outfits and stuff like that. Or the video of one Lady, Carol, that helped girls get "in touch" with their feminine side. (my mom always complained that I'm not girly enough, like there is a scale to judge).

"Being a woman is empowering and if you find it difficult tapping into your feminine side, you can be changed very soon, don't worry," The lady on the screen would start to speak as I would drown her out with fantasies of what a happy life for me would be.

Me and Marissa, running around on a beach with *our* pet dog and then afterwards, going to *our* house. A beautiful house, somewhere hot with a lot of space where we could soak in the sun all day long.

After ten minutes would go by, I would zone back into the video. It would continue on into some story about getting good guys to notice you and making "good life choices."

Thirty minutes of videos would go by and my mother would turn to me in the end, "So what do you think about that? Can you relate to this?"

"Yes ma," I'd say in a bored tone and she'd nod and just go into a long speech on how she was when she was my age. How she used to be this and that.

I'm not gonna lie, it actually hurts that my own mother finds it so hard accepting me for who I am. But, that's okay, Jamie does and that's okay for me.

Since the incident, James and I have gotten even closer and we talk about females from both our perspectives. It is amazing that at least someone in my family got me.

Chapter Eight

After a month of the mental torture and subliminal snide remarks from my parents, the situation just sort of sizzled out. Like she eventually got tired and everybody moved on.

I still got a lesson every so often but as long as I promised to not be a "wannabe tomboy" and "tap more into my female side" (which basically meant wearing all the girly and horrible frilly dresses and skirts and pantyhose my mom always got), my parents would lay off me.

Of course, nothing changed with me.

I was still very gay and continued to be with Marissa, living the life I wanted. We kept our relationship strictly on school grounds to avoid either of our parents finding out which sucked. Even at events outside of school, we'd keep our distance most of the time and just act like "friends" but always managed to sneak in at least one kiss before it ended with one of our mutual friends helping us to keep watch in case someone was coming.

"Be my girlfriend?" I asked her one day after school as we walked to our lockers.

She stopped midstride and looked at me with a confused expression saying, "err… have I been your boyfriend all this while?"

I giggled at her sarcasm and she smiled and said, "I thought we already were already girlfriends."

"I haven't ask you officially, though," I replied, loving the way her words made me feel. She made me feel so wanted and needed and loved. I loved it.

"Doesn't matter. You're mine regardless," she said and that turned me on a bit. It was cute when she got possessive.

Shocked at her boldness I replied, "Wow. Okay then. That was easier than I thought."

"Oh you," she said, punching my arm lightly.

I wished I could have asked her out in a bigger and more elaborate fashion but due to circumstances this was the best I could do. And I didn't dare text her such! We've been very careful with the way we text and we even had to make up some words of ours to confuse anybody that thought to look through our chats.

Our close friends knew about us but not everyone. The word eventually got out around as words did and that was when things started to happen; things started to change.

"Hey Kate, so it's true?" I was asked by someone at least five times a week.

I always asked, "what is?" with an innocent expression, forcing them to finally ask the real question before I'd nod to confirm their suspicion.

Some of the guys were kind of mad because they had eyes on Marissa. Like I've been saying, my woman is just that beautiful.

At first, I only thought a lot of girls were asking me that because they just wanted to satisfy their curiosity. But little did I know how wrong I was. Most of the girls who asked were only trying to make sure it was true before making a move on me. Apparently, a couple of girls had wanted me for the longest time but didn't know they stood a chance because they thought I was straight.

"Well, I always thought you were cute so…" they would say, giggling and twirling their hair and looking at me from under their pretty lashes.

If I'm to be honest, there are a whole lot of cute girls in my school.

"So what?" I'd ask, "you know I have a girlfriend."

This went on for a couple of weeks before I found myself starting to wonder and my mind starting to wander. There were so many beautiful girls… with their long legs and perky breasts and…Urgh, I shouldn't be thinking like this!

I got curious, very curious, about what it would be like to be with another woman besides Marissa. I already know I practically love (hopefully love is not too strong a word but that's the way I feel or at least, that's what I feel love should feel like) and want to be with her but still… there are so many beautiful fishes in the sea and I was still young.

***

By the time the spring came around, Marissa and I were still going strong.

Every morning she would meet me at my locker and we would talk a bit. But this one spring morning felt different.

"Hey babe, guess what?" she asked excitedly.

I chuckled, "whataaaaat? You know I'm awful at guessing?"

"Girl, you're awful at everything," she said jokingly and we burst into a fit of giggles.

"We have orchestra class first today. We can head there now so you can play piano for me before class starts," she said, her eyes twinkling.

"Okay cool." I shut my locker and we walked to the classroom arm in arm.

We saw some people we knew along the way and we stopped for a while to chat.

Once we got to the room we sat together on the piano stool.

"Warning, you might think I'm Stevie Wonder and your heart might melt. I'm that much of a bad ass," I said to her, grinning.

She stuck out her tongue at me and I chuckled.

I began to play a few classical songs for her. She looked me with glowing eyes, which she had done every day we were together.

This made me feel good but mostly bad. This is because of what I knew I was going to do.

Fuck!

I didn't want to, but a little part of me kept insisting and that little part grew bigger every passing day.

I wanted to breakup with her. I don't know if "want" is the right word but I felt trapped. I was just seventeen! And this is the first time I have fully accepted myself and my sexuality. This was the first time I've had girls look at me the way I used to look at them. This is the first time I've had beautiful girls checking me out, giving me googly eyes and licking their lips slowly at me.

I wanted to try out different girls.

Yes, I sound like such a jerk but it just felt like Marissa and I were married. We were always together and not that I didn't love her, fuck, I do… A LOT. But I couldn't just pretend that other girls didn't turn me on. I couldn't pretend like I didn't have fantasies about sucking on Jennifer's ripe, plump lips or squeezing Kasey's huge butt or licking April's neck or having Michelle grind on me. I wanted them all!

I just felt so trapped with Marissa but I loved her still.

I'd told James about this growing feeling and he just laughed and told me, "sis, you a player."

He later explained to me that it was natural. He knew about my relationship with Marissa and always said that it was way too serious for a "bunch of teens."

He told me that it was natural for me to feel the way I was feeling and that it was only I that could make my decision. He could only advise me, but he couldn't tell me exactly what to do.

"Kate? Kate!" Marissa yelled, startling me, "where did you go just now? You looked like someone in a trance."

"I'm sorry, Marissa," I said, abruptly moving my hands away from the piano and hiding my face from her. I didn't want her to see the look on my face. The look of confusion.

She brushed my hair to the side and started rubbing my back, "sorry for what, babe?"

"For zoning out. I've had a lot on my mind."

"Hmm, care to share?" she asked, her face portraying that she only half believed me.

"I...um," I started, not knowing where I was headed. And luckily for me, the teacher came in and the class officially began.

I caught Marissa giving me weird glances during the class and I tried to smile at her. I'm pretty sure I looked constipated.

For the first time, I wished a class could go on forever because I didn't want to have to face her or lie to her.

But eventually, the class ended and as we filed out, she was right beside me.

She dragged me into one of the bathrooms because we had just five minutes till the next class.

"What is going on, Katherine?" she asked.

She never uses my full name unless it was serious and I guessed it was.

I opened my mouth to speak and as if sensing it, she said, "and don't even think about lying to me!"

I sighed and took a deep breath; it was now or never. Looking her in the eyes was the most difficult thing I'd ever had to do in my life.

I took another deep breath and said, "I think we should end this."

And as I said it, the bell rang, signifying that it was time for the next class. Wordlessly, she turned and left.

Chapter Nine

School couldn't dismiss fast enough. I had to talk to Marissa and we didn't have so many classes together. But in the ones we did share, she never even glanced at me. Not once.

Finally, after what felt like eternity, the bell rang, signifying the end of school.

I went to Marissa and asked if we could talk. She was packing her bags and without looking up, she told me to go wait for her in our usual spot. I'd never heard her voice that flat; that void of emotion.

I went on ahead and a few minutes later, I saw her coming. I went to meet her for a hug.

She moved away from me with a confused look and finally said "end what?"

"Us. I think we should break up. I just-"

She turned around and started to walk away but I grabbed her arm.

"I can't do this," she said.

I tried telling her that I loved her but that I was in a dilemma and she looked at me with a look filled with so much disgust that I almost barfed. I never believed that she could look at me that way. It hurt.

"I don't want you to speak, look, or even think about me again," she said in the flat voice, picking up her bag.

"Marissa come on. You didn't even let me finish.".

"Because you have nothing more to say," she said in a voice laced with emotion, "you've said it all."

I heard the sadness in her voice as she said that last sentence and I felt like such a douchebag.

She yanked her arm away from mine with surprising strength and walked away, never once looking back.

For the whole class period the next day, neither of us spoke to each other. Every now and then we'd lock eyes and I tried to smile her but she would just look away with a blank face. She acted like a robot. Her eyes that usually glittered when they saw me were as emotionless as two holes in a wall; almost as if she couldn't see me but through me.

When it got closer to the end of class, I tried passing her a note like a middle schooler, thinking it was some type of cute gesture.

Once the note reached Nat, who was sitting next to Marissa, she tapped Marissa on her shoulder and presented the note. Marissa collected the note, read it for a few seconds and elaborately stood up to go throw it in the trash.

Nat looked over to me and shrugged while shaking her head left and right, knowing I had really messed things up between Marissa and I.

When class ended, I walked over to Marissa. "Can we at least talk about this?" I asked.

"Talk about what. The fuck you wanna talk to me for? You already said what you wanted. A break up? Fine, you have it. You want to explore and whatever, fine. Explore."

"It's not like that," I said, feeling so hurt "I'd rather tell you straight up how I feel than to hide it."

"For months I've been here. I've always had your back and never once saw an end for us but you did. How do you think that makes me feel? You think girls don't hit on me on a regular?" she gave a bitter laugh, "think again, Einstein. But then again we are two different people so, whatever."

"We're so young and I know I want to be with you but I still want to experience everything possible before settling down," I said.

Marissa looked away from me. I knew my words hurt her but they had to be said. She took a minute to gather her thoughts, which led to more frustration on her side. We both took a deep breath and she spoke again.

"I was your first," she paused to clear her throat, as her voice was cracking when she started to speak, "this is real love and you know it. What more do you need to experience?"

"I can't really explain it but I-"

She put a finger over my mouth to keep me quiet, "then there's nothing more to talk about," she said.

She walked away but turned back briefly to say, "stay safe, Katherine Greenwood."

As she walked away, it felt like she was taking a part of me with her.

Fuck, what have I done?

Chapter Ten

From that day of the break up till the end of fall, nothing was the same. School was still going on well but I dreaded going to orchestra class and the other two classes we shared, because I had to see Marissa.

Not because I disliked her or anything, but because I just felt bad. I felt like I just really let her and all of our friends down but most importantly I let myself down. Everyone was rooting for us and our relationship but I ruined it just because I wanted to be selfish, because I wanted to have a taste of different girls. Anytime an opportunity came up, I tried to talk to her but I always chickened out before I could get the chance. It was getting closer to the holidays so I knew it was time to finally say something to her.

Plus, I missed her. I missed her so much. I didn't realize how important our texts and bonding and sharing everything we felt were until they stopped happening. A week after the breakup when I didn't get a single nightly text from her, I was so affected I actually cried myself to sleep that night.

I knew I had to talk to her before the holidays came so, I timed my opportunity one day.

I pulled her aside into the locker room after classes one day, "Marissa, can we talk?"

"I only got a few minutes bab- Kate, Kate. What's up?" she asked. I heard that she almost called me baby and I felt a pang when she said my name. I missed her calling me her babe or her big baby.

"Are we okay?" I asked, knowing we were not okay at all.

"Is there a reason why we shouldn't be?" she asked perplexedly. The truth is that, she was cold. She wasn't mean to me, ever. She was just cold. That connection we shared was gone and I knew it was gone forever.

The fact that I was standing right in front of her and her expression was so blank really got to me.

"No seriously Mari. I miss you."

She rolled her eyes and spoke under her breath, "Here we go."

"C'mon now. You think I'm just over you now? I really miss you."

She looked down and started to laugh, "I don't know, maybe it's the fact that you've been seeing Stacey every day after school that makes me think you are over me now. Or maybe the news I heard about you and April in the bleachers after the basketball game two weeks ago. That was also a way of you expressing your immense *miss* for me, huh?"

I felt a bit ashamed as I said, "okay. That's fair." I said. And it was completely fair. Had I been seeing other women since the break up? Yes. Did it mean anything? Nope. Not at all. I knew this break up would not be easy on either side. I was going to experience other women who I barely liked just to have the experience and she was going to be hurt. But the thing was that she wasn't giving the reaction I expected. Instead, she was acting so blank. Almost like we didn't have history. She was acting like she wasn't the person that I shared everything with. The person whom I ran to when I had any problem and vice versa.

She was polite but very distant and indifferent. I knew she was hurting though, Cynthia told me, but the way she could mask her emotions was almost unreal.

"Yup, you didn't think I knew, did you?" she said, "but then, everyone knows."

She shrugged and told me to have a nice day, walking away with an extra swing in her hip as if to say, "you could have had all this but you missed, bitch."

These types of conversations happened between us a couple of times till they just stopped.

Marissa and I didn't speak directly anymore, there was literally nothing to say and her coldness started making me mad. Like, I know I messed up, I know I fucked up but for heaven's sake, we dated! Anytime we did talk, it was in a group conversation and it was a tad awkward. I knew that she missed me because of the look that would pass across her face sometimes. The look that came and left really fast.

Those looks made me know that we really missed each other.

I continued to mess around with Stacey for couple weeks but I swear it was boring. Everybody that wasn't Marissa was boring!

Us "messing around" just consisted her giving me head in the back of my car after school every day. She loved to eat and she didn't waste time in getting addicted to my taste. Nothing more, nothing less. Every now and then we had casual conversation about school but every time we talked, I got bored. She just wasn't so intellectual and witty; she couldn't make me laugh like Marissa could and we didn't have a lot in common. I quickly figured out that her lips to me were only good for one thing and that made me feel a bit bad. I could she was starting to like me a lot more but I didn't feel the same at all.

I endured until one day I just got so tired of it. She had just finished eating me out and was telling me something about her sister. I swear, I zoned out. The make out was nice, of course, but it lacked flavor. I knew I wanted more but where could I get that if not from Marissa? I thought about this every day I spent with Stacey till I ended things with her.

Luckily, she's bi and was on Timothy Rando's cock like we didn't even happen.

Next up on the roster was Melanie.

"So…Stacey huh?" Melanie, one of Marissa's closest friends, approached me one day after school.

"Um, huh? What do you want?" I said, smiling as I shoved my textbooks inside my locker. I looked at her from top to bottom twice and I liked what I saw. She was mad cute and automatically, the flirt in me got stirred up.

"I heard what you've been doing in that new car," Melanie said, leaning a hip against the locker. A lovely, well-rounded hip.

"What about it?" I asked, shutting my locker with a snap.

"I think you know…" she said, giving me the most seductive eyes ever and slowly biting her lower lip.

"Maybe, maybe not. But assuming I know, what would Marissa think? Are y'all still friends?"

"Yes. But what she doesn't know won't hurt her," Melanie said in a husky voice, her pupils dilating a little.

This whole encounter taught me that friendships really don't mean anything sometimes. Melanie had been "close" friends with Marissa since middle school and she knew about our relationship. Hell, she was even one of the people rooting for us. But obviously, a cute face and nice smile was all it took to betray a friendship…She was willing to stab her friend in the back for me.

What a crazy bitch.

"Okay, barbie, I'll see you tomorrow… at my car," I said.

And nodding, she slowly kissed two fingers on her right hand and placed it on my lip. Turning to walk away with an extra show just for my viewing pleasure.

The sneaky friend fantasy shit was hot as hell at first, but just like all the others, it didn't last long. Melanie's girlfriend, oh, did I mention she had a girlfriend as well, was not very happy when she found out about Melanie and I.

"You need to check your best friend!" Melanie's girlfriend, Shawna, sent to Cynthia on social media.

When Cynthia told me, I was in a troublesome mood. It was time for a nice virtual fight. What else did I have going on?

"Is there something you want to say me?" I posted.

"I don't like you. No one does," Shawna replied underneath my post.

"But your girlfriend do… or rather, her mouth do. *A lot.*"

After I sent that, all hell broke loose.

You could tell I won this round with Shawna because her only reply was a dm to me stating that she wanted to fight. Many girls, over time, wanted to fight me but never had the full courage. I feel like my mysteriousness and general calm was the reason.

No one had actually ever seen me fight or get mad so they had no clue to what to expect. This made me happy, seeing as though I couldn't even hurt a fly…I hated and will forever hate violence.

I saw that Marissa was online but she was focused on Kasey's page. Even though I knew nothing was going on, I was jealous.

Chapter Eleven

In the fall of my senior year I received my college acceptance letter. It wouldn't be long before I head down south to attend college. I wasn't as excited as I thought I'd actually be. When Marissa and I used to date, we'd often talk about how excited we'd be when we finally got into college. We'd get so psyched about how we'd leave this "boring" high school. But right now, I wasn't all hyped up because a great part of me was going to miss high school. Not high school really, but Marissa. Even if we didn't talk so much anymore, almost not at all, seeing her brightened up my day. Literally.

But there were some serious advantages, really serious ones that kind of trumped my high school nostalgia. The fact that college presented me with new opportunities, new friends, the fact that nobody would really know who I was and that I would meet a LOT of beautiful girls from all parts of the world. Those were major points but the trump point was the fact that I didn't have to deal with my parents every day anymore! I wouldn't wake up to my mother's subliminal look of disdain or my father's constant indifference to every single thing to things that didn't pertain him directly.

As I packed my bags for the first of my journeys away from home, I looked around and felt fine for once.

"Well this is it," my mother said with a soft sigh. I couldn't tell if it was a sigh of relief, or if she was actually going to miss me. I looked at her for a long while. I *really* wasn't going to miss this woman. Not at all. I was only going to miss Jamie. I'd miss him a lot.

My parents stared at me for a minute or so, anticipating some type of speech or a dramatic performance perhaps of how I'm going to miss them or the home or something. But my face was just blank and expressionless. I didn't have any words at the moment though and even if I did, they surely won't be words of sadness or regret because damn, internally, I was jumping for joy. For the first time in my life, I can make my own decisions openly. I can wear whatever I want to wear, eat whatever I want to eat and most importantly, be with whomever I want to be with. I always thought it was weird when other people my age get super sad when leaving their parents but I had to realize that not everyone had the same experience with theirs as I did mine.

My dad broke the silence, "make good decisions and make sure you stay around the Career building office. You need to get a good job when you get out," he said while giving me two awkward shoulder pats. What a horrid man.

I finished bringing all of my bags in from the car and laid them on my dorm room floor. After unpacking a few bags, my parents and I stood there in silence again. It was clear that it was their time to go but no words were being said. No tears, no long speeches or talks about what to expect from school, or sappy hugs and cheek kisses, just silence and I think my mother was about to tear up.

Urgh, what a dramatic and pretentious woman. Like she'd miss me.

When it was clear that they intended to mope at me for the rest of the day if I permitted, I gave a false smile and said,

"Alright, I need to finish unpacking. I want to see if I can make it to the bookstore today. It'd be really good if I could get all the books I need today."

I saw a look of approval come into my father's eyes but go immediately. I wasn't going to miss this.

"You want us to come with you?" my mother asked. My father lightly grabbed her arm and mouthed, "let's just go," to her.

"Okay," she said, "we're going to head out."

She came in and gave me a hug as my father patted me on the shoulder again and gave me an awkward side hug.

"Be good," they both said while walking out the door.

As soon as the door shut, I cried. Not because I was sad but for the first time in many years, I felt a weight lifted off my shoulders. They'd always been around, causing my mental state to decline and I was never comfortable.

I wiped away my tears and started to laugh. The first real laughter I have had in years. This was my room! I immediately ran to my suitcases. I pulled out a t-shirt, sports bra, and a pair of cutoff shorts that I made from Jamie's old jeans. After I slipped into this comfortable outfit, I slid out the new pair of Jordan 1s that I had been hiding from my parents for a few weeks and danced around with them.

"Ooh la la! All mine!"

Moments like this made me glad that I didn't have a roommate. Having a place to be alone and carefree, without worrying about my parents or brother entering without permission, was one thing I really looked forward to when school started.

I still had a good amount of time to unpack and gather my things before heading to the bookstore so I walked around the hall a bit. I wanted to take in my surroundings and so far, I loved the weather.

"Yo! Kate, right?" A girl at the end of hall got my attention, "It's me, Brittney. I sent you that direct message a month ago."

"Ah okay. Yea. I remember," I said, pleased that at least, I knew someone. Even if we didn't talk much, I wasn't going to be completely stranded.

"You unpacked yet?"

"Not really. A few things here and there but I just want to explore the campus a bit, see the walls."

"I'll come with you," she said. I wanted to be alone a bit but I figured I should be more open since I am in college now.

Chapter Twelve

I thought I found love again after a month or so in college.
    Okay, that sounded super dramatic. Let me rephrase. I thought I found someone I could vibe with an be with. To put it simply, I thought I found another Marissa.

Yes, I know that sounds crude and unfair but I couldn't help it. Marissa had set the bar really high and I found myself looking for her in everyone else I met.

Anyway, about this new girl, her name was Jade and she was super sweet to me.

I first met her the second week of school while we were still in the orientation "get to know other students" phase. She was 100% straight but that clearly didn't stop me from falling for her. She was a babe and more.

With her beaded braids that brushed her waist, her septum nose ring and her glittering skin that shone like it was made of the finest caramel. She looked like a chocolate, like a human chocolate bar.

"Who in here knows Jade's boyfriend?" I asked my new circle of friends. Thanks to Jade. Her friends literally adopted me into their circle and now, we were all really close.

"Kate please don't. You got enough girls, gay ones, that need some of that attention of yours. I know Jade and she is not with that. Relax," Sanai said, while the others nodded and agreed with her.

I roll my eyes at Sanai, she was really mouthy and I liked her for that. Making friends with these girls was my first step in trying to get the girl I wanted. My foot was already in the door with Jade by befriending them.

"I'm not with what? and why should Kate relax?" Jade walked in suddenly, causing everyone to quiet down. "C'mon ya'll. Spill it!"

"Look Jade, you already know what it is so I'm not even going to stress it," I really thought I sounded smoother than warm butter in this moment, "You know of me and I know you so maybe we-"

"Kate what the fuck are you even talking about?" Jade said, with confusion. Everyone laughed and looked in my direction to see nothing but a blank expression on my face.

"Nothing Jade, she's just tripping," Sanai shook her head and continued on with the night. "Who has the bottle though? Vodka, scotch, brandy? I need a few more shots before we head out."

"You're such a lush, Jade! We are going to a party! And we just downed a bottle of vodka, plus I caught you sipping on your 'party brandy' you keep in your flask," Lakeisha, a sassy girl with natural pouty lips and big hazel colored eyes exclaimed, making us all burst into a fit of laughter.

The girls went to the mirror to touch up their hair and makeup while I stood there silently trying to think of how I could get Jade to like me. I knew that I should just let her be because she clearly wasn't like me but I couldn't. She was that straight girl that I wanted.

The summer breeze brushed against my skin as I stepped foot outside with the girls. Something about that warm air gave me some more much needed confidence to reach the, or at least what I thought during that time, girl of my dreams.

Jade stood next to me the whole way to the party and I tried to make conversation. "You gonna save me dance?" I asked Jade as we got closer to the party house. Already, I could hear the sound of music and screams from excited youths.

"Hmm maybe. We'll see," Jade winked at me then walked up further with a little extra swing in her steps to join her friends. Women like this kill me. Such teases. I loved to dominate them. Have them writhe under me in pleasure.

"What does that mean?" I asked but Jade could no longer hear me because of the distance between us.

An hour went by fast and already, I was slightly tipsy. The party was growing stronger and there was all the types of booze there and weed.

"You're definitely not going to get anywhere by just staring at her," Sanai laughed, passing me a joint.

Damn, this shit good.

"Just watch me work, Sanai. It might take time, but I'll break her walls. I've broken the walls of tougher, mouthier women," I said the last sentence looking Sanai directly in the eye. I saw her face flush a little but she immediately controlled it.

Sanai rolled her eyes at me and walked away.

I chuckled to myself, remembering the way she had pounced on me like a hungry lion. Yes, Sanai and I have made out before.

I smoked my joint some more while I watched Jade. I was going to ask her for a dance again, but not yet.

If I'd admit, the fact that she was straight made my attraction more intense. She was something I couldn't really have, but really wanted. Another thirty minutes went by and I finally decided it was time to dance with Jade.

I looked around the room to find Jade only to see her walking back towards a bedroom with some guy and I groaned.

. "Urgh, and there she goes…" I said to myself.

"You're Kate right? I met you the first week. I'm Lindsey," a sweet, slightly nasal voice said behind me.

I whipped around and looked her up and down trying to remember who she was, "okay right. Yea Lindsey, I remember," I said knowing good and well that I was lying. I couldn't for the life of me remember who she was.

I sat down as she said, "dance with me," and before I could even process what was happening, she sat in my lap and started grinding on me. Feeling her soft body on made me feel better. Her ass was really soft and I found myself rubbing the small area of her back. I wanted to squeeze her buns but I had to control myself. Plus, a part of me was still trying to figure out who the hell she was!

"You like that?" Lindsey asked sultrily.

As if knowing, the DJ started playing all the slow jams. Lindsey couldn't have come at a better time. *I just wanna take it nice and slowwww.* The DJ had to be reading my mind playing that good Usher. This song never fails to get me in the mood.

"Let me get your number now before the night ends," I said to her with no hesitation. She grabbed my phone and put her number in. Looking at her, she was pretty cute but I doubted I'd call her anytime soon. I know who I really want.

A few more minutes went by and I saw Jade coming out the back room. She saw me looking at her and walked towards me, a big grin on her face.

"Hey Jade," I said gently, rolling my eyes at my stupidity. Urgh, like she could actually hear me over the loud ass music.

"Don't look like that. I never forgot I owe you a dance. You still want it right?" she asked, practically glowing. That guy must have been something.

There were a few things I wanted at this moment but I guess a dance would suffice.

I chuckled lightly. "Yea. Let's go," I said, allowing her pull me up.

She was a great dancer.

Chapter Thirteen

"Tell me you love me babe."

"Okay. I love you, Jade," I said and I wasn't exactly surprised when I felt the slap land on my cheek.

"And I'll do it again if you don't say it like you mean it," she bucked at me and stormed out my room.

There was nothing more I could do then to laugh it off. I became used to it. I thought I deserved it after a while. I told everyone I loved her and that she was the one for me. And I really wished she was sometimes.

Yes, Jade finally accepted me.

It took a lot of doing but she became mine. It started at that party. During the dance, I found out she was an awesome dancer and so was I. We bonded so much on the dance floor, especially during the sensual dances. It was truly amazing. The way we touched each other was something to see.

After that, we started talking more, like so much more and the more I got to know the real her, the more I liked her. I don't know when she started really liking me, but two weeks later, I felt a drastic change in our connection.

We were constantly together and I loved her wit. She was also a sight to behold. So beautiful.

One day, we went to a park and when we were on the swing, I told her how I felt.

How much I'd liked her from the first day and how she was the reason that Sanai and the rest of them are even my friends. I mean, I loved them, but I would have never accepted them or talked to them if I didn't want to get Jade.

While I talked, I heard sniffles. She was tearing up.

"Oh gosh, Katherine," she said and my name sounded like sex coming out of her mouth. My actual name, not Kate.

"Oh Kate, nobody has ever gone to that extra mile for me, I don't… I don't know what I'm feeling right now, honestly. I'm straight… I mean, I just broke up with Jason and I've never *ever* been attracted to any girl in my life before. But with you, something has changed in me... I find myself wanting you, thinking about you… I don't-," her voice cracked as she broke into a sob.

I held her, wanting so badly to kiss her but doing nothing of the sort.

Jade and I spent majority of the day and night together so much more after the incident and I noticed that she would flush shyly each time she saw me before we got comfortable again. Having a single room made it a lot easier for us to have alone time throughout the day and we would just cuddle up and watch movies on my laptop and smoke some weed or read our books or drink. I preferred pot to drinks, I can focus with pot and still be super productive. I can be even more productive with it than in my sobriety.

Eventually, Jade and I had our first kiss.

We had just seen a movie, it was a sad movie with a happy ending and when we were celebrating, she just sort of jumped on me in joy and I gripped her waist and went in for it. I couldn't control myself anymore.

She hesitated for a few seconds then with a sigh, she wrapped her arms around my neck and returned the kiss with intensity.

After that day, things almost got awkward, but I persevered and eventually, we started dating.

Along the line, I started getting bored. I don't know why, but most girls can't hold my attention. Only Marissa successfully held my attention like a pointer dog with very little effort.

Sometimes I wanted to be alone but didn't know how to communicate that properly without Jade getting offended.

Being with her, I realized that Jade was quite bossy and extremely attention demanding. It was cute at first but now I was getting bored, it had become a bore.

It was a rainy Tuesday night when I decided that I just couldn't deal again.

Looking at her, I saw that tonight had to be the night. I wanted to be done with this shit.

"I want to be alone tonight," I said to Jade as she walked into my room like she owned the place.

"I see you didn't notice my new purse but okay. And I don't understand what you mean," she said.

And I suddenly got so irritated.

"I just want to sleep alone. We can chill for a bit but I want to be alone. You gotta go, love," I said with a smile.

"Hmm, so you're tired of spending time with me? Huh? Now you want to be alone?" she asked in disbelief.

I rolled my eyes exasperatedly and said, "we're together every night, Jade. You have stayed her every single day for over three weeks. I've never asked this. This is literally the *first* time I'm saying this. There's no need for us to fight."

She quickly walked to me and started to swing her hand back then forward towards my face. I caught her right before it touched me.

"Hey!," I shouted, "get out of my room Jade. This violent bossy shit is so outplayed and I could break your spine if I wanted to. So quit it!"

I wasn't joking. My parents made Jamie and I take Ju jitsu and Taekwondo when we were younger. I was pretty damn good.

She folded her arms, getting angrier by the second, "it's like that now, huh?"

"yes," I walked over to the door and opened it, "I'm not even going to fight you right now. Just go."

If looks could kill, I'd be dead from the look she gave me and she slammed the door so hard a painting fell down.

What a drama queen.

Chapter Fourteen

Jade didn't talk to me for a whole week. She neither called me nor did she text me and that was just okay by me. It was funny how I didn't even miss her, funny how she didn't cross my mind.

While I rested on my bed after a hard and long day of lectures, my mind couldn't help but wander.

It wandered around all the girls I've dealt with. It was funny how I didn't have any romantic feeling towards any of them. It was funny how every single time I met someone new and eventually dated or had a fling with, I subconsciously compared that person to Marissa.

And it's safe to say that none of them even come close to being as good as she was.

And then there was Jade.

Honestly, I have to end things with her the next time we meet. I'm not cut out for all the drama. I just want a warm, willing and pliant, soft bodied woman that will succumb and submit to my every sexual whim.

But was I ready for love? A part of me argued that I wasn't, that I still wanted to test the waters. But another part pointed out to me how happy I was when I was with Marissa.

Sure, we were younger then but I'll be damned if the love we shared wasn't strong.

I'll be damned if-

My train of thoughts were interrupted as I heard a loud knock on my door.

I was tempted to keep mute; I wasn't in the mood to receive guests. But the knocking persisted, and after a while, I was forced to drag myself off my bed and went to open the door.

"What?" I say before I realized that it was Jade standing in front me then, "oh hey stranger. Havent seen you in a minute, come on in."

With the controlled look on her face, I could see that she was trying so hard to contain her rage. I saw that the chirpy and cheerful tone in which I used to welcome her grated on her nerves and she felt like giving me a huge kick in the nuts (if I had nuts, that is.)

She sat down on my straight-backed sturdy chair and I could see how heavy her chest was heaving. One of her sure signs of madness. *Oh boy.*

"So err… what's up, Jade? You look good," I said, looking at her with an appreciative glance.

"Oh really? I look good huh? And that's why you haven't said a word to me in two weeks! For two whole weeks, Kate, you haven't even cared whether I live or die. What is wrong with you? Have I done anything to deser-" she started heatedly, but I had to shut her off before it escalated into something else. I had had a stressful day and I didn't want to transfer any sort of aggression to her.

In my household, my parents made it a point to always heap up all their pent-up aggression and frustration from work and of course, their next destination was home to dump it on my brother and I.

I know how terrible it feels and I wouldn't want to do that to another person but this girl was pushing me to the wall.

"Look, it's enough!" I finally scream, for the first time.

I saw the startled look of fear jump into Jade's eyes and that fear turned to uneasiness after a few seconds.

"I have had it with you and your constant nagging. I don't do this, I don't do that! Fine! Go and fucking look for someone to do all of them!! Look for someone that you won't have to yell at daily to get your point across."

"But K-" she started again, in a more subdued voice but I was already so far gone.

I told her that I didn't love her and that what attraction and fondness I did have for her died when her nagging became unbearable. I told her about how she nags for every little thing and how unattractive a quality that is. I even pointed to her how she tended to get violent sometimes.

"Look, I'm tired of this and so are you. It's best we go our separate ways right now. We can't keep fooling ourselves this way. Come on, let's be realistic about this."

The look on Jade's face was so comical I would have laughed out loud if I didn't know the gravity of the situation.

"You are breaking up with me? You are breaking up with Jade Peterson?" she asked as though I had blasphemed.

"yes, I am," I said unbothered.

"you will pay for this. I hate you!"

With that, she ran away and slammed the door. That was the end of it for us.

Chapter Fifteen

A few months later, my life took a dramatic turn as usual and every free moment I had I spent in apartment 1421-C.

That was where Tyra stayed and where I spent most of my time.

Oh Tyra.

I had met her about a month ago and it was a very dramatic but almost cliché meeting.

I had some assignments and projects due next week but I just wanted to get it done with so that I could be free.

My hands were loaded with books I was going to return back. The moment I bent into a corner, I walked smack into someone carrying as much load as I was. Then, when I bent down to get my books, she did too and our hands touched the same book before we looked up at each other.

I was struck by her.

She wasn't your conventional beautiful girl but she had something. This magnetism that made her sensual and irresistible. And that was exactly how I found her; sensual and irresistible.

We giggled shyly and when we straightened up, she looked directly at me and gave me a small smile before she scurried away.

From that day, I made it a duty to always visit the library. I quickly discovered that she had a favorite spot at the library.

I started talking to her. Slowly at first but then the more I got to know her, the more I knew that I wanted it to be more than friendship. I don't mean love, not at all. Or maybe I did at that point.

Anyway it took close to two weeks of steady wooing and I got her eventually. The chase to get her wasn't as exciting as Jade because Tyra is bisexual but I felt like the queen of the world when I won her because she was always the "hard to get" type.

But the good thing is that we weren't official. We were together, but not official.

***

I heard my phone buzz and smiled when I saw Tyra's text.

"When are you coming over?"

This text always gave me déjà vu every time I read it. Tyra sent me that text every day right after her classes were over. I would head to my dorm, grab my phone charger, keys and a change of clothes and walk right over to the local apartment complex.

And my heart would start beating heavily as I got closer to the door to 1421-C. It even gave me more joy that the door was always unlocked for me.

Just for me.

I would come in, set my things down and head straight for Tyra's room. She really knew how to treat me like her queen. Having a friend with benefits was normal at our school. Being able to spend time with someone you like without the commitment of valentine's day dinners, daily check-ins and long reassuring text messages at 3am sounded good to the average person.

Less than 2 minutes passed and she was already undressing herself. There were times I did just want to chill and talk but Tyra always wanted a piece of me, always.

She would feel and touch my entire body from head to toe. Slowly. At first with her hands, then her tongue. With every touch I would get wetter and wetter. Feeling her warm skin against mine made me feel whole. Not that I was missing anything in life or she filled a deep void, no, she just made me feel complete in those moments. Now don't get me wrong, I still had other women on my line.

A lot of girls wanted a piece of me and even some guys tried to "convert me." Getting with women was not a problem for me but something about Tyra just felt right. She would kiss me like I was all that mattered in the moment, touch me like she was trying to learn my body, always cum for me like I was her first, and moan my name like it is the sweetest sound in the world.

Chapter Sixteen

"What's on your mind, baby?" Tyra asked one day after we just had sex and I had just dressed up.

"Nothing Ty, it's just been a long day and after what you just did to me, I can barely even feel my legs."

But as I looked around, I knew that there were so many things I wanted to tell her. So many things. It's funny how easy it was to talk to Marissa.

Part of me wanted to mention to Tyra how her occasional pillow princess act was getting old. The pink décor and the ultra barbie shit was getting on my nerves too.

But an actual truth was that Tyra, although having been sweet and nice couldn't please me sexually. She was too much of a receiver and not a giver. Having sex with her was like having sex with a rag doll.

And, I'm not proud to admit that when I wasn't with her, I was with someone else who actually got the job done. It seemed like a waste at times to please someone who doesn't do the same to me back but it was worth it with Tyra. But still, I just *had* to have my release.

But naturally, I'm a giver. I am a person who gets pleasure from pleasing others. Getting to know another woman's body is so fulfilling. Getting to explore it and drive the said woman wild was something I enjoyed doing. That's why I was still down with Tyra.

Tyra's body just spoke to me. Every time we did it, it felt like the first time. She would moan, giving me confidence that I really knew what I was doing. And of course, I did. But, I wouldn't get the full release I wanted.

Oh well, you can't have it all, right?

Tyra didn't know my friends much. They didn't roll with the same circles or know much about each other which was better for me in a way because Tyra had no idea how many girls I'd explored, Tyra would just have to put up with my past if it comes up anyway. After all, I never claimed to be a virgin.

I refuse to get caught up in any drama involving women. I've been in enough trouble as it is.

"Kate when you coming over?" Tyra texted me one day, but little did she know, I was already on my way. She followed up with another message,

"Actually wait, I have a SisUnited meeting tonight so I might not be home when you get there and I wouldn't want you to be stranded outside."

SisUnited was an organization at our school. Some sort of organization that deals with females looking to expand themselves on campus and reach career goals. She sent that text a little too late because I was already walking up the steps to her apartment. The knob was ice cold with this terrible weather but I still grabbed eagerly, ready to see Tyra.

I opened the door and there stood Kayla.

Kayla was this really cute girl in my biology class. I crushed on her at a point, but I just took my eyes off her because she was just so… prim. She was the type of girl you have to think twice before walking up to and spewing trash. But we did maintain pretty heavy eye contacts during lectures.

A room could be filled with a thousand people and I'd still be able to pinpoint Kayla. She just stood out to me with her beautiful glow. We locked eyes and smiled.

"Kate! I need to talk to you real quick," Tyra said, interrupting that ethereal moment while pulling me to her room.

"Okay Ty slow down. What's up?" I asked, a bit startled by how almost hysterical she looked. She took a little look outside her bedroom door before closing and locking it.

Looking anxious she said to me, "did you get my text? Why do always ignore my messages?"

Her aggressiveness was so uncalled for and for a moment, I just stared at her. Blinking as I was lost and short of words.

"I didn't look at my phone. I'll just go. Hit me up after your meeting," I said flatly and as I made to leave, she stood with her back to the door and asked if I was mad at her. Women are super confusing sometimes. Like what does she want? Was I meant to cry or something?

"Did you do anything to make me mad? ," I asked with a chuckle, "I'll go."

She raised her head for a kiss and when I pecked her lips, she smiled and moved away from the door.

Right as I opened the door I saw Kayla was standing right outside of it.

"Sorry I was just looking for Tyra," she said while locking eyes with me with those slightly slanted beautiful and enchanting eyes of hers.

"She's in her room but, how are you? Feels like we haven't talked in a very long time."

"Kate, we shouldn't do this," Kayla said, a flush starting to creep up her neck and unable to meet my eyes.

"Do what? What's wrong?" I continued and smiled to lighten the mood.

"I have a girlfriend now. You might get me in trouble." I was still confused but this did boost my confidence up a couple notches.

"But I literally said nothing?" I said and when she had nothing to say, I shrugged, but my confidence level was still on hundred percent.

I didn't even come onto her and she was ready to risk it all for nothing. Like she couldn't resist me. Hehe.

"Okay Kayla."

I said, giving her a very seductive look to let her know that it's far from okay. And while I walked away, I felt her eyes on me till I couldn't feel them no more.

What is wrong with me? Why did I enjoy flirting with another woman in my own woman's house?!

A little voice in my head whispered, *because you haven't found what you are looking for.*

Well maybe, maybe not.

Chapter Seventeen

I saw Kayla again on Friday night. She was in the cafeteria with her friends, just as I was. The special of the day was "Honey glazed roasted duck" and it was so good, the cafeteria was packed. Later on that night, we would be going to our first real college party. Every freshman was going so I knew she would be there.

"So where is this party at though? I know it's gonna be so lit," Brittney said while watching the cafeteria workers add mac-n-cheese, followed by fried chicken, to her plate.

"Extra cheese, please" we all chorused, knowing that she'd ask for more and we burst into a fit of giggles because we were dead on.

"I think it's in the student center. Where else would it be?" Desiree asked.

Dana interrupted, "Naa ya'll we in Holbrook's tonight. Ya know... *the Holbrook,* the gym."

My heart started to beat faster. So it was true, back in high school, I used to hear tales about college parties they had in Hollbroks. Everyone drunk, high, and hot as hell letting loose on campus.

"All I know is one of these niggas getting their life rocked after this party," Brittney said flipping her hair.

"Bitch bye! The only thing you rocking is a sad ass face the next morning when that nigga kicks you out!" Dana said, causing laughter to erupt from our whole table. My friends never failed to give me a good laugh in the cafeteria. I glanced around a few times to get a quick look at Kayla. I saw her siting alone with another girl. It was clear they had some type of intimate relationship by looking at their body language. Or maybe I was just seeing things because I was falling for her. I knew that I had to end it with Tyra. I was already so bored and I'm sure she is tired of my nonchalance.

Still I'm not worried because what I feel now for Kayla is real. Well, at least I hope it is. This is what I always tell myself but so far, it's just been a series of monotonous conversations and wild sex.

I'm not a nympho, but I don't know why I just can't seem to be with one woman for a long while.

"Alright Kate be honest please, do you like my fit or what?" Brittney asked. Brittney and I always made sure to help each other out with party outfits before going out. We had similar fashion

"Yes girl, you look good," I said. Brittney always looked good, honestly.

Out of everyone in my friend group, she was the only one guaranteed to catch an eye. Basically, she was bad as fuck. I probably could've had a crush or something on her but she was too much of a friend for that. I didn't want to ruin a good friendship. Plus we almost did something once, and that was what made me vow to always draw the lines with my friends, no matter how beautiful or gorgeous they are.

A few weeks ago, we were alone in her room picking out outfits for an occasion. I asked her, "What if I liked you? Could you see us doing something?" I looked away as fast as I could to not create any awkwardness between us.

"I mean... what would our friends think?" she said, still looking in my direction.

I walked toward the closet door, as to create more space between us in the room.

"I'm not sure what they'd think but I'm just being hypothetical."

She paused for a moment and started to walk towards me.

I could have gone, I could have shifted but I was curious and a bit turned on. I wanted to see what she'd do, what she was up to.

When she came to me, she leaned in close and I grabbed her waist and leaned in towards her neck. She lifted my head up slightly with her left hand and kissed me. I pulled her closer and continued to kiss her back. It was a nice kiss and my hand slipped into her shirt to fondle her full, heavy breasts. I kept sliding my hand in slower till a knock at the door startled us. We both moved quickly away from each other and Dana busted through the door.

"What is in the world is going on in here!" she said, suspiciously in a shrill voice.

"Nothing is going on, girl, what is wrong with you?" I said calmly. I was surprised by how calm and expressionless I looked (I caught a glance of myself in the mirror.)

Dana stared at us for a couple more minutes than nodding, she came in. She texted our friends that evening and they all came over.

Safe to say that Brittney and I denied that anything happened. I don't know how we did it but we eventually convinced them otherwise in two hours.

After that, Brittney and I promised each other to never do it again. Every day forward, we acted like nothing ever happened but I never forgot and I know she didn't too.

On the way out with Brittney and the girls, I realized that I *had* to end things with Tyra, as soon as possible.

Chapter Eighteen

"I got your text,'" Tyra said the moment she entered my room. She didn't even knock, she just barged in like she owned the place.

I was laying on my bed, playing a game on my iPad and from that angle, I could see the fleshy part of her thighs through her short skirt.

Funny how I wasn't fazed by it.

Seeing her like that would have given me shivers in the past and the lust in me would have been flamed, but right now, I just wanted to get this over with.

"How was class today?" I asked because I had nothing else to say. I could see that my silence was beginning to bother her.

"Great, yours?" she answered, coming to give me a peck.

I got a whiff of her scent, lavender, a scent that was just peculiar to her alone.

Am I going to miss her after I've done what I have in mind? Maybe, maybe not. I don't know, I'm not thinking that far. What I do know is that I have to end this relationship with Tyra.

It's so unfair dating her and having fantasies and dreams about Kayla.

Funny how time flied. In my freshman year here at college, I never believed that I would even be opportune to date someone like Tyra.

I didn't see her coming in my wildest dreams. But now, not only did I have her, but I was bored with her and on the hunt for someone exciting and new.

I don't know what exactly my problem is. I have been through a sea of women but for some reason, none of them can interest me for more than a few months.

It's like there is this switch inside of me that just turns itself off at will. So that when I like a girl, I could just stop liking her so suddenly, so abruptly.

Looking at Tyra as she walked around my room doing this and that, I couldn't help but remember when I first started crushing on her. She filled my every waking moment.

She really excited me but now, all I did see were her flaws.

Like the way she chewed with her mouth open and noisily, the way she acted when girls she thinks are better or richer than her are around. The way she…

"Um hello!" Tyra shouted, pulling me back to reality and out of my imagination, "what is wrong with you, Katherine? I have been talking to you now and you are just blank."

I blinked twice, coming to, "I'm sorry, I travelled. Or rather, my mind did."

I saw her nostrils flare a bit and a faint flush come to her cheek. Uh oh. Bad signs.

Those were telltale signals that she was getting pissed.

If she's this angry now, how will she be hen I tell her the sole purpose of her visit? Yikes!

"Um…" I started, clearing my throat softly, "sit down here, please."

I patted to the space on my side.

"Wait, babe, if it's to ask me to go the upcoming event with you organized by the Caveman Fraternity, the answer is duh. Fuck yes. Who else would I want to go that kind of rave with?" Tyra said, flipping her hair with a little attitude.

I knew the event she was talking about and I even looked forward to it.

The Caveman Fraternity were one of the biggest and richest fraternities in school. Their parties are always the best and students always look forward to them.

Hell, even students from other schools in the community come for the Caveman parties hence, it was a must-not-miss!

And boy, did I have plans for that day. Only, they didn't include Tyra.

"That's great, but that's not the reason I called you. I-" I started to say but Tyra interrupted me again.

"You are creeping me out babe. Are you sick? Did something awful happen?"

I hold onto my temper with an effort and say, "no, Ty. Nothing happened. I sent you that text to come over because I wanted to talk to you about us."

I saw her stiffen and a wary look jumped into her eyes.

After a moment, the look is replaced by one of resentment, understanding and cold acceptance.

"Don't tell me, you want to break up, yes? You have suddenly discovered that we are not compatible and you want us to go our separate ways," Tyra said in a flat voice, echoing exactly what I had in mind.

"Um…yes? Well, Ti, it's not like that. It's-"

"It's nothing, Katherine Greenwood! It's fucking nothing. God, I saw this coming! My friends warned me. You have a reputation for being something of a womanizer and a lady killer. A reputation of seducing girls, making them feel like they are the Queen of Sheba and then turning around weeks later to dump them and on to the next best girl," Tyra said in one breath, her voice rising with every sentence.

I winced a bit. Her voice could travel but I was happy that the rooms were somehow noise proof.

"Please, calm down, Tyra. It's not like that, I swear."

"You swear?" she asked, jumping up like the bed was on fire, a murderous gleam in her eyes, "you swear? Fuck you! You know, I thought that ours would be different. Sure, I'd heard the tales, but I'd deluded myself that ours was different and you loved me for real. What a fool I'd been. You are incapable of loving anybody but yourself and yes, your exes think so too! Yes, word travels and I sure as hell have heard some stuff. But I was thinking ours would be different. I was thinking I'd be able to tame you. But I see that I was wrong. Nobody can tame you. You are a horrible, horrible heartbreaking bitch and I hope you die!"

With that, she flipped me off with both her hands and angrily walked to the table where she kept her bag.

That doubled as my dressing table and before I could do anything, she pushed everything on the table onto the floor. My creams, colognes, oils and other things came crashing down with a loud noise.

She broke my flower vases and before I could register what was happening, she turned back and screamed that she hoped I burn in hell. With that, she was out.

I looked around my room and felt like a heel. I saw that she had broken my most expensive Hugo Boss cologne but I didn't mind. Not really.

I kept thinking of all she had said and with a feeling of dismay, I saw that she was right. I didn't know how to love and I had been playing games with the hearts of all the girls interested in me.

But I didn't do it on purpose!

When I start to date, I'm really completely immersed in that person but along the line, something changes.

It starts to feel wrong and I feel the likeness I have for the girl disappearing… I can see it but I can't do anything about it. The way water pours out of a basket is the way my likeness fades until there is nothing left anymore.

I sighed and went to get a broom.

At least now, I could fantasize about Kayla in peace without feeling guilty. With that pathetic thought to keep me company, I started sweeping up the broken glasses on the floor subconsciously noting that I must have broken Tyra's heart the same way.

Chapter Nineteen

The party was a big as I expected it to be. Hell, it was even bigger.

The moment I stepped foot into the big darkish hall that was occasionally lit up by shiny disco lights, I got lost in a sea of bodies, loud music, booze, drugs and energy.

The Caveman Frat always outdo themselves each time they throw a new party and this was no different.

The party was at capacity and more people were still coming.

I had decided to come alone because I had been asleep when my friends called me to come get dressed with them.

Now, I wasn't exactly in the mood to party but I knew that I had to attend this one.

After a lot of talks, my friends reluctantly agreed that I could come on my own. I'd meet them there and after the call, I went right back to sleep.

An hour later, I was up and 25 minutes after, I was on my way to the frat house.

"Where r u guys @?" I texted Brittney the moment I got there.

"By the left side of the DJ. First floor."

I picked my way to my friends. It was a packed house party and I had to occasionally push someone aside or break up a make out session and after about a billion "excuse me(s)" I finally got to my friends.

"Look who showed up, sleeping beauty," Nicole said loudly over the music.

I greeted everyone and Dana pushed a cup into my hand. I didn't even ask what was inside, I just took a sip.

"Who wants tah smoke?" Nicole asked after we had all been cruising for a while. We all squealed in unison.

She excused herself and came back a few minutes later with a fat blunt. I handed her over my lighter and opened my hand to collect it back immediately after she lit the blunt.

She raised an eyebrow up as if asking "why?"

And I said, "I don't trust you bitches with my lighter. Nuh-uhn. Each time I bring a new lighter, I never get it back. I really love this one and I'm making sure as hell it follows me home today!"

The girls looked at each other and started laughing.

"You're insane, Kate," Dana said, taking a drag from the blunt.

"A real trip," Arabella agreed.

When the blunt got to me, I took a drag and savored the way it went into every crevice of my body.

I was already getting a bit tipsy from the alcohol and decided that later on, I'd switch to just fruit punch. I didn't want to get drunk, I just wanted to get high.

I hoarded the joint until Brittney screamed, "hoarder! It's puff, puff, pass and not puff, puff, I'm keeping you all to myself forever."

Everybody laughed.

After a while, we all dispersed to go have our individual fun.

I didn't really come over for the party. I just came by to get high and let loose. That's what I told myself, and of course, I was deceiving myself.

I knew in my heart that the major reason I came here was because I thought I'd see Kayla and the thought of seeing her did something to my insides.

I was heading to the kitchen to mix myself another drink and to roll a joint and it was almost comical how many girls I had to say hello to before I got to the kitchen.

Tyra's words came back to me with full force and I grimaced. I shook my head, trying not to think about one very heavy truth she mentioned.

I am a womanizer. I'm a play girl.

My train of thought is interrupted as I hear a loud, familiar laughter that came from the kitchen. I was two steps away and when I walked in, my suspicions were confirmed.

There were a couple of people in there, some had slumped from too much drinking, others were bat-shit drunk and others were just mixing their drinks.

Tyra was one of the others getting drinks for herself and I saw that she was with Callie Calloway. Callie Calloway was a really beautiful girl and her father was one of the chair people on the school board. That made her super popular and super arrogant.

She had her arm around Tyra's waist while Tyra mixed the drinks.

When I walked in, they both looked up and I saw a look come into Tyra's eyes before it quickly disappeared. A look of longing.

"Hey girls," I said. I was already pretty high and Tyra meant nothing to me. At least nothing more than a fast fading and distant memory.

They murmured greetings and I went on ahead to roll a joint from the big glass jar filled with pot and rolling papers.

While I rolled, I felt Tyra's eyes on me and I noticed that she kept touching and caressing Callie. She would then laugh unnecessarily loudly at everything Callie said. That was when I confirmed that she was just trying to make me jealous.

I chuckled out loud but immediately covered it up with a cough.

They finished and left. I didn't even know that had gone till I turned around and didn't see them anymore.

I rolled a couple of joints and mixed a big ass drink.

I was going to the dancefloor. I didn't want to dance, I just wanted to sit on the comfortable looking couch and watch people dance.

I wanted to be entertained.

I feel like Tyra was monitoring my every move because the moment I picked a spot for myself where I could have an uninterrupted view of the dance floor, she went onto the dancefloor with Callie.

Now, when it came to dancing, nobody was better than Tyra. She knew how to move her body really well. No doubts.

She was dancing so seductively with Callie, some of the other dancers shifted to give them space. She was really drawing the spotlight onto her and I could see that her face was focused in my direction.

I grinned to myself and just when I thought I'd had enough, I saw Kayla walk to the dancefloor by herself.

I knew Kayla was beautiful but that little black dress she wore on her body was something to see. She looked sculpted, perfect.

I settled more comfortably into the sofa and focused all my attention on Kayla.

Looking at her dance, the fluid graceful movement of her body and the way she cleverly put the guys that came up to dance with her in their place, my attraction for her intensified.

She was really a beauty to behold.

Chapter Twenty

Kayla texted me, "come over at 12pm. We need to have a really serious talk. But, I'm not in the space to have it at this very moment but when I am we need to have it."

Now what did she want to talk about?

While I waited for 12pm as it was just 9:47am, I thought back on how Kayla and I got to where we are today.

I have to admit, getting Kayla was so much more difficult than I thought it would be.

I could even go as far as saying that she was the most difficult girl in my life that I'd had to trap. Trapping her wasn't easy at all. I remembered how it all started.

"Black dresses are made for you," I said to Kayla the Monday after the Caveman Frat party.

"Huh?" she asked, blinking and I could see that she was genuinely confused.

"I saw you at the party on Saturday. I saw you in your little black dress. I have to say that you stole the personality of the sun that day because you looked way hotter."

"Oh," she said and after a moment, she giggled, "nice try, Shakespeare but your lines are a bit too corny. Try harder next time." With that, she was off.

I was a bit taken back. I didn't know that she had this much attitude in her, this much sass. I didn't know she was feisty like this.

I loved the fact that she wasn't an easy pushover that anyone could just get at. So, I had to work to get her attention, huh? Alright.

A part of me squealed in excitement at the prospect of having to hunt; to chase her and win her.

I realized a while ago that I love to win my girls. I feel better when I work hard and win a girl's heart than when a girl just says yes on the get go or give me green lights because she already likes me.

It is more fun, more of an ego booster wooing a girl that claims that she is hard to get and getting her. I love that shit.

Anyway, after that, I started making it a point of duty to talk to Kayla when I see her. All the time, everywhere. I thought this would work, I thought it would give me the leverage I needed to win her, but I was wrong.

Kayla was not like other girls, not really.

She didn't like the fact that I would stop her all the time or talk to her every single time. She once yelled at me for being a "stalker creep" and told me to "get lost."

She had a terrible impromptu test that afternoon and was in a bad mood. I happened to appear at that time and I was used as the emotional punching back for her transferred aggression.

She apologized the next week, and that was how I knew what really happened.

Anyway, I toned down on the contact. I realized that with Kayla, subtlety was the way. She would rather I maintained eye contact with her in a packed cafeteria than me walking all the way to her table.

She loved to be teased and what was I, if not a master in the game?

Gradually, she started talking to me. We would sometimes meet at the library and have a long talk about school work and everything.

I loved the fact that she was really smart. It damned near drove me crazy. I loved the fact that I could talk to her about anything. She would understand or have a little knowledge of it.

I started really liking her more than I anticipated and after one day, as much as I hated to admit it, I discovered with a little shock that I liked Kayla so much because she was so similar to Marissa!

No wonder I liked her so much. She was so like Marissa. More like Mari than any other girl I'd been with.

They had the same cleverness, the same poise and this touch of elegance. This air of being prim, proper and classy.

The discovery was both a shock and not a shock. It was a shock because, duh! And it wasn't a shock because my subconscious had noted it from the very first time I laid eyes on her.

It took me talking to her and wooing her every single day for way over a month before she finally accepted me. The day she accepted, I kid you not, we popped a bottle of champagne.

We had our own private party in my room as I'd already moved out of the dorm.

I had gotten an apartment a couple of months ago. A little sitting area, my room, a little kitchenette and then the bathing area. It was super comfortable and spacious and I loved it completely.

Kayla was the first girl I had sex with in my new home and that was on the day she accepted to be mine.

I checked my watch and it was 11:30am. How time flies.

I pulled into Kayla's apartment complex and ran up the steps to the fifth floor. I was so eager, I didn't even want to waste time waiting on an elevator.

I knocked twice on the door a few seconds later, she came to open it.

I liked her a lot but I was quick to discover after close to two months of dating that I didn't love her. Not at all.

I liked her so much but I didn't love her. That initial attraction I had mistaken for love faded after a month but I did like her. At least I liked her more than every other person I had dated in a while and that counted for something.

"Hey, what's going on? How was your day?" I said to break the silence.

She walked to the kitchen area and pulled two glasses from the cabinet.

"It was fine," She said while pouring two large glasses of red wine for us. She handed me a glass and a sat down at the table. I sat down across from her, wondering what was wrong when she suddenly blurted, "I think we should end this."

Chapter Twenty-One

I felt my heart stop for a minute and just start up again. Did she just….

"Err," was all I could say because I didn't think I was hearing right.

I was still waiting for more emotion. There wasn't much expression on her face but I didn't want to assume the worst. I didn't want to believe that I heard right.

"Stop looking at me like that, say something!" she said finally hysterically, looking at me. She was wringing her hands together. That showed that she was agitated.

I was the one getting dumped and she was the one getting agitated. If the situation weren't so dire, I would have laughed.

"What do you what me to say?"

"Say something, say anything. Don't just sit there and stare at me like I'm a doorknob!"

"You are ending the relationship with me, Kayla. Why are you yelling? Why are you yelling so much when I am the one getting dumped?"

"Stop saying *dumped*, Kate! That's our problem now. Stop saying that." She took a couple sips of wine to calm herself and I did the same.

I backed up from the table a bit and looked away from her with confusion, "what do you want me to do or say then?! Okay, fine. Why? Is that what you want to hear?

Fine, I'll bite. Why, Kayla? Why are you ending things with me?"

She looked at me incredulously. Even though my voice and character were laced with sarcasm and mockery, a huge part of me really wanted to know *why*.

Is this how it feels? To be dumped? I suddenly remembered the plethora of girls I had broken up with and I felt even worse. I felt like a fucking monster.

Like an emotional fiend.

"Fine, fine," she said while looking down and rubbing her forehead head, "I know you're an asshole but I'll be honest with you. The why is because I don't want the inevitable ending. The part where you dump me. I don't want that. Trust me, I love you Kate. I love you so much. I love you with an intensity that scares me most times and it hurts. It huts so much because you don't feel the same way. Shh, don't argue. I know you want to argue with me, but in your heart you know I'm right. That is your M.O, K. Everyone knows you."

She takes a pause to catch her breath and I'm reeling. Listening to all she's saying and hating her because she was right.

"You're like a drug, Kate. A drug that every girl wants to have a taste of and every boy wishes he could sniff. Once you get in a girl's head, she becomes addicted to you and then you can do whatever you want with her and walk out anytime. Now, I don't know why you enjoy using women because you're a really great person, an amazing human being. And… I'm getting addicted. I can't afford to get addicted to you, Kate. Because we both know how it would end. I lay at night in fear waiting. Waiting for you to drop the bombshell and the wait, Kate… the wait is driving me insane. I can't do that no more, I'm sorry."

I still said nothing. In a way, I understood her and was really proud of her. Proud that she was strong enough to let go.

I could see it was killing her. I could see all the telltale signs of her agitation.

I took two more sips of wine before I looked over to her, "are you sure this is what you want?"

She nodded and closed her eyes, "I promise I tried, Kate, I fucking tried but I can't do this again. I'm too scared. Sorry, Katherine."

Never before had my name sounded so beautiful coming from her mouth, oddly. It came off smooth but cut me deep like fresh razor blades. The room was silent but her words continued to echo so loudly to me.

"Okay, babe," I said and I saw her flinch a bit at the word *babe*. The sadistic part of me enjoys that but it's soon gone.

I stood up and pulled her up with me, giving her a hug.

I gathered my things and walked to the front door. Before I let myself out, I turn just in time to see a tear slide down her left cheek. I feel my heart breaking and I feel a type of pain I'd not felt in a long, long time.

"Thank you for being honest with me, Kay."

With that, I shut the door gently behind me.

Chapter Twenty-Two

Getting over Kayla was not easy, I can't lie.

I don't know if it's because I liked her or if it's because she was the one that did the breaking up and not me. Yes, I know that sounded awful but it's what it is. My ego is at stake here.

In all my rendezvouses, I was usually the one that called things off. I was the one that decided that I didn't want a relationship anymore and the girl would scramble around or go find someone else. I called the shots. That dom in me always took charge.

But with Kayla, it was the other way around. She had called the shot and it was driving me crazy. It made me want her more, it made me miss her more and it made me dwell on the fact that Marissa was the reason she meant that much to me.

Which means that it made me to think about Marissa all over again. Shit, shit, shit, shit oh, I'm sorry, did I forget to mention shit!

My mind had been a mess and I was just trying to get a hold of myself because exams were coming up and I had a fear of failure. My scores alternate between As and Bs and I'd love to keep it that way.

After the second week of the breakup, I had to have a serious conversation with my damn self. I had to tell myself that I needed to SNAP OUT OF IT!

I started with doing lots of exercise and yoga. I found that exercising helped me transfer my anger unto something and I did it with deadly determination. I enjoyed it so much because when I was at the gym, everything seemed to fade away.

My friends thought I was hitting the gym hard because I wanted to have my "revenge body." They were so wrong but right in a way because my body did start looking more banging. I started eating healthy also, and meditation, which eventually led to proper mental healing. I did see Kayla once in a while and it was awkward but hey, that's life right?

After a month and a few days, I was almost over the whole thing. If I could have gotten over Marissa (which I know I really haven't but let's not open this can of worms), I don't see that woman that I can't get over.

Two months go by and I got a text one day that read,

"How are you?" My heart skipped a beat and started to pound. After the break up, I had deleted Kayla's contact so I wouldn't be tempted to check on her, but I knew her number. This was her number.

Is this really her? She's thinking about me? Does she miss me now?

I replied, "I'm chill, you?"

She went on to tell exactly what my subconscious thoughts wanted to here, "I'm okay. I miss you, honestly."

Then I searched my heart and found out that I didn't miss her. At least, not anymore. I didn't want her back. But she would always hold a special place in my heart though.

"Nothing?" she texted after waiting for some minutes and getting no reply from me.

"What do you want me to say, Kayla?" I replied, giving a tired sigh.

"I want you to say the truth, Katherine. For once, say the truth," she responded immediately.

"The truth can hurt, Kayla," I finally replied after a few minutes.

"Oh. Oh, wow. Okay," she texted.

She got the memo; I didn't miss her too.

In a way, I was glad that Kayla happened. I really limited myself around girls. I mean, I was still crazy and I still had them, but just not as much and the ones I did have, I made sure to treat them good and always be honest with them upfront.

It's funny how many girls will still fall for you even knowing that you just want sex.

Chapter Twenty-Three

I was super eager for the skype call to connect. It felt like I hadn't seen Jamie, my brother for a million years.

"Yo, rugrat," Jamie's thick voice oozed out of the microphone.

"Big brother!" I screamed wildly, making him burst into laughter. After a minute, he joined me and we just kept screaming and making noise and laughing for some minutes before we quieted down.

"I have missed your crazy ass, Jamie," I said honestly, because I did.

"The same here, smurf. I have missed you too. Nobody to steal my clothes or disturb me."

I laughed and then we started talking about different stuffs. His new girlfriend, my conquests, school, his job and really everything.

"Have mom and dad visited you since that last time?" I asked my brother. I didn't want to talk about my parents but I had to ask Jamie.

Jamie had moved out of the house around 13 months ago. It has been a crazy time. It was so crazy that even I in school felt it.

Of course, my parents didn't want to hear anything of it. They didn't even believe he had gotten an apartment until one day my mom wanted to do laundry, she went into his room (which he forgot to lock as usual) and she found out that more than half of his clothes and things were missing.

When he got back that night, he told them that he really did get an apartment and they were livid.

They said that he was irresponsible and not ready to handle an apartment which was a laugh because Jamie worked for his money and paid for it himself.

I swear, sometimes I called him "dad" because he could act so old.

After a heated week, the parents finally saw that they wouldn't win this one and reluctantly allowed him to go.

A month later, they went to review the apartment and after that, they never went back or saw Jamie again till date.

"Well, no… but mom called two days ago, she said she'd come this weekend. Sunday, that's in two days to bring me homemade meals and stuff," Jamie replied.

"Mom wants to bring you homemade meals?!"

Jamie laughed at the surprise in my voice, "I was surprised too, rugrat. Trust me. But that's not the case. How are you preparing for your finals?"

I rolled my eyes and entered a long conversation of why I hated school and why I loved it.

Ahhh, finals.

It felt like just yesterday, I was a freshman. Today, I'm in my final year and would be due to graduate in some months. I was doing my first semester exams. Just one more semester and hello world.

I was both excited and scared.

***

"Bobby-Joe MacPherson!" the dean shouted and after a lanky, tall guy came up the stage. All smiles with his graduation gown and big cap that almost swallowed his long head. That was Bobby-J alright and today was my graduation.

After four years, I was finally done with college.

As I sat down there, I was swamped with different emotions. I was excited, scared, and just a number of strange emotions.

I looked at my graduating colleagues; they were nervous but I could see that happiness and fear. In a way, we all looked the same. We were all young adults who just graduated college. For fucks sake, we weren't even young adults anymore.

We now had our lives ahead of us. And that was a scary thought. Not to be bound by the shackles of nature.

"Omg, my mom!!" a girl beside me said happily and turned to wave at a woman that was all smiles and tears away from us. It was so cute how many parents turned up for this ceremony. There were so many mothers and siblings in the crowd, tearing up. For some students, their entire family came. Like Bobby-Joe, his whole clan was around.

I looked in the crowd for my parents, they weren't here. They didn't come.

I smiled and silently thanked Jamie. I had to make him promise not to tell mom and dad that I was graduating today. I knew they wouldn't check the internet or didn't really care, but my parents did this thing where they had to "do the right thing" just so that "people won't talk." Not because they wanted to, not because they were moved, but just so that people won't think they don't care. Which they don't.

I didn't need them here.

Besides, they would want me to run home with them immediately and that was the last thing I wanted. My rent still had like 8 months before it was due and during that time, I wanted to figure out what I'd do. Do with my life, do with my time.

I knew that going back home was totally out of it. Nothing, not even the promise of getting an autograph from Rihanna would make me go back home! Not yet, at least.

The dean droned on until I heard, "Katherine Greenwood."

There was a sound round of applause, especially from my friends in the crowd. I was aware that all eyes were on me but I wasn't shy or scared. I was hungry and just wanted today to be done with so that I'd go home and get high and eat pizza with hot chocolate while watching *Scandals* for the 100th time.

I walked to the stage and while I was handed my certificate and the pictures were being taken, I looked at the crowd for real.

Oh my, what a huge ass crowd. The fuck? I ain't even know the crowd was this large.

Aww, look! Jamie came!

I saw my brother was filled with joy. The fact that he drove all the way here was just too sweet and I was just-

Oh my goodness!!! Is that Marissa?! Was that Marissa I just saw or are my eyes playing tricks on me?

As I went back to my seat and the next name was called, my eyes kept scanning through the crowd like a crazy person. I could have sworn that I saw Marissa!

Fuck am I hallucinating or was that real? Wasn't that Marissa? If she was the one, then why didn't I fucking see her again? If that was her, then where was she?

Did she disappear?

For the duration of the ceremony, I had to control myself from turning around so much to scan the crowd.

After the main graduation ceremony, the dean and members of the school board left to allow the students do their thing.

Some of the graduating students were in different frats so for that day, a huge party was organized by all the frat house to honor their members that were finally done with this school shit.

I found my way to Jamie and gave him a bone-crushing hug. That is if he wasn't over six inches taller than me and way huger.

"I can't believe the rugrat is finally a woman," James said all smiles.

"Oh, shut up. I can't believe you came! I'm so excited, Jamie. You know you didn't have to," I said with feeling, hugging him again.

"Hey, hey," he said, holding me, "you know I wouldn't miss this for the world."

I thanked him again and thanked him for not telling on me to mom and dad. That was the best gift of all. The gift of his silence.

We decided to go to one of the numerous food-stands around to get barbeque and liquor. While we ate, I heard a voice say over the loud music,

"Damn, I thought this bitch was gay? What's she doing with such a hot nigga?" I snorted and almost spat out my drink.

"Do you have to be so loud?" I asked Candace even before she came into view. She looked really beautiful in her red dress and I told her so.

Jamie was grinning and pretending that he wasn't noticing or enjoying the admiration in the eyes of my friends.

Jamie was actually something to look at. He was around 6'3 and had everything necessary to drive a girl crazy. And his new tattoos didn't make it any easier to resist him.

He had that masculine thing; that bad boy goodness that drove a lot of girls insane and looking at Candace, I could see that she had already thought up 64 positions she and Jamie could be in.

"Well girls, this is my brother. This is James. and Jamie, these are my friends, my girls, the reason I've been partially sane all this while," I said eventually.

The gasps that followed were funny.

"Girl, tell me you're joking," Nicole said in a low voice that only I could hear.

I nod my head "no," and she went "wow."

I could see the disbelief in their faces and I was suddenly so proud of my brother.

Yes, I know it sounds vain, but who wouldn't.

"Um, Kay, these seats aren't gonna be enough for your friends," Jamie said and he stood up. I swear, I virtually heard all my friends' panties drop when they saw Jamie in all his glory.

"Come sit here," Jamie said to Nicole who was closest to him "I'll go get more chairs."

I know she has dark skin but I swear, Nicole blushed. She sat down comfortably and I could see the little jealousy in Candace's eyes. She wished she were the one Jamie offered his chair to.

I laughed privately. This might just be a fun day after all.

That is, if I could get Marissa out of my head.

Jamie came back with more seats and when we were all seated, we ordered more food.

It was so sweet to see how my brother got along with all my friends. He saw that they were subconsciously competing for him and he had to make sure every girl feel special. He divided his attention amongst them in such a way that nobody was lacking and nobody felt cheated.

He didn't show any preference even though I could see that he was staring at Arabella way more than usual.

She didn't notice it, but I did.

I knew Jamie too well. He knew how to do this thing where he could stare at someone and the person would never know. It was a skill on its own and I saw him checking out Arabella quite a lot, which was funny because amongst them all, Arabella was the one that didn't really gush at him.

I mean, she looked at him because, duh. But she wasn't all that psyched like the other girls.

I looked at her some more. I did like her. She was really cool and blunt and I could see why Jamie was looking at her.

Arabella had this class that just couldn't be bought. She didn't try too hard like the rest of them girls. She never did. She didn't wear makeup; she was too lazy. She didn't go crazy about the latest fashion and shopping. She just didn't push her femininity in your face. And she was fucking sexy.

I crushed badly on her at a point but she's completely straight and she talked senses into me. That was when I started respecting her even more. She gave me some good tongue lashing.

I knew that my mind was travelling, but I liked her for Jamie. Really, I did.

"Hello!!" Nicole said, snapping her fingers in my face. I was so lost in my tipsy thoughts that I didn't even know what they were talking about.

I blinked, "what did you say?"

She rolled her eyes and everyone laughed.

"Where did you travel to, madam?" Nicole asked.

I grinned and said, "South Korea."

"You dumb shit," Jamie said and we all laughed again.

We were all tipsy and happy.

"I said what are your plans? I mean now, you're done?" Nicole asked again.

Closing my eyes and leaning more comfortably into the chair, I answered,

"really, I don't know yet. I haven't exactly thought that far, have you?"

She shrugged and shook her head.

"Yo, let's not think about our futures, right now, okay? It's a scary thought and let's just vibe and focus in this moment. The right now. We have our whole lives, literally in front of us. So, for now, more drinks and ribs!" Arabella said suddenly, breaking the awkward silence that got too real because none of us had shit figured out.

We all clapped and cheered.

I sharply looked at Jamie and I noticed something like admiration come to his face for a moment, then it was gone. But that one glance was enough. Arabella impressed him.

I looked at her as she went to get the drinks. She was wearing a simple off-the-shoulders short back dress. It had long sleeves that stopped at the knuckles and it was tight but not skintight.

She had a thin gold chain around her left ankle and black flip flops. Her toe nails were painted white, she wore no makeup and her septum piercing kept getting caught by sun the sunlight. She wasn't trying at all, yet she still managed to look sexier than all the other girls. I was proud that she was the one Jamie was going for.

If I were in his shoes, she'd be my choice too.

"Okay, what's the time? It's 5:47pm, I'm beat as fuck," I said, yawning and stretching.

"You know we still have to go to the after party yeah?" Emily said and I nodded.

We decided that we'd go home and have a little rest, change and then meet at the Caveman Frat.

"I hope, you'd be there, James?" Nicole said as we all stood up, gathering our things.

"Um, I planned to actually drive back tonight," James said, a sorry look on his face.

"So, you won't be there?" Arabella asked and I saw Jamie stiffen.

"He'll be there," I said, and I nodded when he looked at me, "he'll crash at my crib and drive back tomorrow."

"First good idea you're making, ever," Emily said jokingly.

"Ain't that the truth…" Candace agreed and we laughed.

We waved and kissed goodbye. All the girls, except Arabella, gave Jamie a hug. She stood where she was and waved to him, "see you tonight, *Jamie*."

I saw my brother grin. He liked that she called him Jamie. Normally, he never allowed people to call him Jamie. Well except for me and a few other old friends.

While we walked to his car, I kept looking at him and grinning.

"Okay, what gives?" Jamie finally asked as we drove to my apartment, "you been looking at me like a freak that you are, fo sho. What happened? I have paint on my face? What's up?"

"Nothing, *Jamie*," I said, mimicking Arabella. I knew he was going to ask about her. I was just waiting for him to bite.

He talked about this and that till we got to my place.

"Nice shoebox you got here, smurf," Jamie said as he entered my little apartment.

Before I locked up and went to keep my stuff in my room, I saw that he already found my ashtray and some unfinished joints.

"Good to know this is what you use the cash I send you to get, good to know," he said, taking a large inhale.

"I learned from the best," I said, winking at him.

"But then though, this some dang good nug," he said. And when I made to take the joint he held, he whisked his hand away and said, "roll another one."

"But it's finished! I don't have no pot no more," I whined.

"Yeah right," he snorted and after I saw that he wouldn't give. I hit him in the belly and went to get my stash from the room.

"Liar liar," he snorted.

I rolled two fatties and while we relaxed, he finally asked the question I'd been waiting for.

"So err… your friends are chill. What' up with that Arabella chic or what's her name?"

Finally, I knew I wasn't crazy!

I busted into laughter.

"Hey! What gives? Why you laughing?"

Mimicking him, I said "*or what's her name?* oh please, Jamie. You're so full of it. I saw you looking at her. I have been waiting for this question since the car."

Realization dawned on his face, "aha, that's why you were acting like a freak."

"Will you deny it?" I challenged.

After a while, he grinned and threw his hands in the air, "alright, you win. I do like her. Found her hot as hell. She looks kinda different from the rest, y'know?"

"Yeah, I know. Like she's not trying so hard but somehow, she's still better than the rest of them," I said and Jamie grinned at me.

The grin was so sincere as if to say, "now, you get it!"

He snapped his finger at me and I snapped mine right back.

"Yeah brother, I get it," I said and he nodded.

We talked some more about it and I was really glad Jamie came. I was glad that I had my brother around on one of the most important days in my life. It was really great that he came all the way to see me, really great.

We talked until it was time for the party and got dressed and left.

Chapter Twenty-Four

Okay, life after school was not what I thought that it would be. I thought that it would be all chill and I'd have all the time in the world to myself.

And one of those assumptions were correct; I had all the time in the world to myself, no really, I did. I had so much time on my hands, I was going crazy. Yes, crazy with fucking boredom. Heck, how do people stay home all day long for years?

By the third week, I was already tired of myself and bored out of my mind. I was so bored, I thought I was gonna climb the wall.

The school was mostly empty, the session was out and students had gone home. I never go home and my parents were already so tired of asking me to come home that they finally took the hint that I wasn't interested and they gave me my space.

My mom at one time had the audacity to accuse me of trying to avoid her, of trying to avoid them.

I was so high that day, I couldn't even bother to be polite or pretend like it was nothing and I blurted out, "yes! Yes, I'm trying to avoid you. Yes, I'm trying to avoid a house where every single move I make is contradicted or where nothing I do is good enough. A house where I am constantly compared to people I know nothing about! I'm tired of being treated like an option. Like a mistake. I'll stay in school, thank you very much."

The shock on my mother's face was something to see when she said, "oh, I didn't know you felt that way. Very well then."

I replied, "well."

And that was the end of the conversation. So much for a mother that really wants to bond with her child.

I kept thinking of what to do. I knew that I couldn't take any more of this staying idle all day long thing. I knew that eventually; I'd have to do something. But what?

I majored in finance so I could be anything from an accountant to a banker to whatever, but the thought of working from 9-4/5 really bored me.

The pay would have to be exceptional for me to take that kind of job.

"Urgh, I guess I'd do my laundry right? Better than being cooped up in here all day. I'm going fucking mad," I said, talking to Penny.

Penny was my new cat and she was adorable. Penny was a stray cat that would usually come into my area and sun bathe herself in my apartment complex. I liked her independence as I'd watch her from my window every day, idly.

Eventually, I started leaving treats for her by my windowsill. Treats like milk or tuna or fish sticks. After a long and patient wait, I finally won her over. I was the only human in the area that she would allow pet her and a month ago, I said, fuck it and adopted her.

It was really great having her around and I'm sure I might have gone out of my mind, literally if she wasn't here.

While I moved around my room gathering all my clothes that needed washing, Penny licked herself and looked at me with her pretty green eyes.

"You're so beautiful, my sweet," I said, coming to rub her belly and she purred loudly.

Such a spoiled brat. She loved to be pet.

I put all my stuff in a big bag, loaded the bag with detergent, bleach and soap. I got my headphones, a joint, my lighter and my phone. With Penny hanging on my shoulder, we headed downstairs to the laundry room.

There was a laundry room downstairs with four washing machines in there for the residents. I got there and luckily for me; it was empty. Not many students were around and even if my building wasn't located inside the school, it was dominated by students and it was 70% empty.

I was washing my second round of clothes, stretched out on one of the three plastic chairs available with my leg on top of the long wooden table located inside the laundry room, stroking Penny's fur (she was perched on my lap) and smoking my joint with no care in the world when someone suddenly came in.

"Oh shit," I said, putting down my legs and immediately putting out my joint, "the landlord isn't in and I didn't know anybody was even around right now. Sorry about the smell of smoke."

"Um, it's fine…" the brown-eyed girl said and came fully into the room, placing her basket of clothes on the table.

After sorting her clothes and popping them in the machine, she said to me, "you don't have to stop smoking on my account."

"Alrighty," I said and set fire to my joint. I was watching her through my peripheral vision and I saw that she was watching me.

"Um, want a drag?" I said after a while, I felt like the silence was a bit awkward.

"I'm not much of a smoker. I'm not a smoker at all but seeing as there's nothing to do and I'm almost mad with boredom, why not?" she said, stretching her hand to get the joint but I don't hand it to her.

"This some pretty heavy stuff. Are you sure you want to try it? I don't want you freaking out on me neither do I want to be that bad influence neighbor that gave you drugs."

I didn't see pot as drugs, trust me. Not in any way after all, it grows from the ground, doesn't it?

To my surprise, she started laughing, "it's not that serious, *mom*. Plus, I wanna try it, so give it. And don't get me wrong, I've smoked before. I'd just rather drink."

I pass the joint to her and finally asked after she stopped coughing from the first two drags, "what's your name? seems like you're new here."

"My name's Jennifer, and you're…"

"Kate," We said my name together, at the same time.

"How did you know my name?" I asked her.

"Well, I'm new here, but not really. Juke is my friend. I hang in his room sometimes and I see you from his little balcony sometimes. You have these pair of amazing purple Nike slides and I just had to ask him one time who you were when I saw that shit."

I grinned, I loved people that had a keen eye for fashion.

"Well, it's a pleasure knowing you, Jennifer."

I was typing on my phone when I said that and when I didn't get any reply from her, I looked up.

The next thing I saw made me want to choke with laughter. It took all the willpower I had to not.

She looked like someone that had seen a ghost and her eyes were so red.

"Are you okay?" I asked her, knowing what was wrong but choosing to play innocent for her pride and so I wouldn't embarrass her.

"Well, you were right. This is pretty heavy duty. I'm trying to convince myself that I'm sitting in a chair and the sound I'm hearing is the washing machine, and not me flying through the air. Because that's exactly how I feel right now. Like I'm flying through space and the sound is the sound of the wind."

I couldn't hold it anymore, I burst out laughing.

"Oh wow, that was impressive. You got a way with words, I fuck with that," I said and she gave me what was meant to be a wrong stare but came off goofy because she was too faded to be mad at me.

I grinned at her and told that she was handling herself pretty well and that she should try not to be paranoid. I convinced her that I was with her all the way and I guaranteed that I wouldn't let anything happen to her.

I could see that she was really grateful that I was patient with her and in four hours time, long after we were done washing, we were still down there talking and laughing like we had known each other for years.

She was still pretty high because she was taking occasional puffs. She enjoyed it so much that she literally begged me to go roll another one when we were through with the first one. She said that I had a very soothing effect and that she felt safe around me.

Well, what do you know? She feels safe around me.

I don't know why, but hearing those words made me feel really good.

It made me feel on top of the world. I guess I'd been bored for too long and been too occupied with thoughts of Mari and sometimes Kayla.

It's funny how a week after my graduation, I still caught myself looking outside and hoping that I'd see Marissa. I guess the reason was that I checked her out two days before my graduation.

I couldn't take it anymore and I had to just know what's up with her. With it being the age of the internet and social media, I couldn't help it when I did something I swore I'd never do and didn't do, except for once.

I checked her out on social media. And it was my mistake because goddamn! Marissa grew up fine! I thought she was beautiful in high school but judging by the Instagram photos I saw without filter, she looked so much finer. So much finer, so much finer than I remembered she was in high school. And you know her face was planted in my memory bank for life.

I was a bit jealous to see that she had moved on with life and was clearly living her best life. From what I could see, she was a writer (wow, you know I have a thing for people with words! Couldn't she be something else like an Instagram influencer or something that silly and vain? Why did she have to be a creative and impactful writer?!) and a speaker. I couldn't imagine an audience that wouldn't be captivated with Mari.

I know it's a vain thing to say, but her look alone would hold anyone's attention. Urgh, I have to get over this girl. It's been what since we broke up? Like six years? Seven years? What the actual fuck is wrong with me?

"So, are you down for some shots tomorrow?" Jennifer asked as she stood up and stretched. Looking at her now, she was quite adorable. With her big brown eyes and her silky brunette hair. She looked mixed, like part African and part…Lebanese? I didn't want to ask her. It'd seem a bit insulting or whatever, what with everybody in the world right now trying not to be that "racist fuck."

"Um, let me check my calendar for my schedule," I said and pretended like I was consulting a calendar as I looked at my palm seriously, "well, young lady I might be free to squeeze you in from 3:15 to 3:25pm, how's that?"

It wasn't that funny, but she was pretty blazed and laughed like it was the funniest joke in the world. Was this girl a confidence booster or what?

Urgh, Kate.., get a grip of yourself. Everything feels like a confidence booster to you these days because you have been single as a peanut.

And it was true. I had been single for close to two months and it was so awkward for me. I was never without a girl and now, I had nobody. A lot of girls still hit me up on social media, especially girls from school. Girls in classes lower than I was that knew I was still going to be around. I don't know how, but words flew around pretty fast in college.

But I didn't want them. I don't know why, but even glancing at their messages and profiles had me yawning with boredom and starting a conversation or continuing one was way too stressful.

"See yah, Kate," Jennifer said with a wave as she strutted out of the laundry room.

My tummy growled, but I ignored it for a minute. Was it me, or was there a more obvious swing to her hips as she walked out? Excuse my question, but did Jennifer want me to check her out?

Don't play yourself, girl. Sis was probably just too high and in too good of a mood and besides, you don't know what she walks like so what the hell is your problem?

I chuckled to myself, it's funny how I berate myself more than any other person in this world.

I looked around for Penny, I didn't see her. I had even forgotten that Penny existed. But Penny being Penny, she was probably already waiting for me in my room. She would have gotten in through the windowsill.

I knew that was what would most likely have happened, but I was still kind of worried. I loved that damn cat.

***

"Oh my goodness," Jennifer exclaimed, breathing like someone that just ran a marathon, "That. Was. Incredible! I mean…what the…where did you… just wow."

I grinned at her. She looked really cute with her hair all tousled up from the hot fuck we just had.

This is one little freak I had lying beside me. Damn, she almost ruined me.

I was a bit proud of myself, okay, maybe more than a bit. I was super proud of myself. I still had it.

I still had the skills to drive a woman crazy. I know it's weird to say, but if I'm being honest, I felt really good.

I had been feeling shitty because I still hadn't figured out what to do with my life and it's been two months since I graduated. Some of my classmates already had jobs and incredible lives and seeing their fancy and sweet and happy posts on social media just made me want to curl up somewhere and weep.

I wasn't short of cash. That's something my parents made sure of, and so did Jamie. Also, I had a job.

I did some freelancing jobs online. A little painting here, a little picture editing there, a little consulting here and there. I discovered that I loved being a consultant. I loved helping people put their lives in order even if mine was a big pile of mess.

Helping others manage their lives, businesses, finances and any other thing they needed kind of gave me a grip on life.

I decided to occupy my time by learning how to make dope pasties and edibles.

"So, what are we going to eat this night, babe?" Jennifer asked me as she stood up and stretched.

"Um, at this point, I'm down for whatever," I said feeling satisfied and snuggling into my pillow. Jennifer and I had started having sex three weeks ago and it was funny the first time it happened because two days before that day, she kept convincing me that she was straight.

Apparently, she and her boyfriend had decided to "go on a break," (scoffs, what a joke). And this happened after she had caught him in a compromising position with another girl. She had been so devastated when that happened.

She told me that she had kissed a girl before, but that was when she was in high school. She hadn't had anything to do with any other girl again.

Except me.

We made plans for dinner and she said she'd come back to my house in an hour. She blew me a kiss and left. It was great having her around.

She was a great conversationalist which is like gold these days to find. Having her around, there was never a boring time. She always had something to say, and that was fine by me. I didn't have much time or patience for people that would always wait for me to initiate the conversation.

Eventually, it happened. What I feared would happen happened. After two months with Jennifer, I was bored!!!

I was so glad that we didn't define what we had. We were never in an official relationship, although I could see that she was liking me way more than she bargained too. There was an off chance that I could like her so much as well but the thing was that… she was too clingy, way too clingy. I mean, we lived in the same building. Her house was just two floors below mine and I swear from the moment this girl woke up, it didn't matter if I was awake or not, she always came by. That is, on the day she doesn't sleep over. She was one of those people that had never heard the phrase "distance makes the heart grow fonder."

In her own case, distance was a taboo.

If it were possible, this girl would sew herself to me like my Siamese twin. She was always in my face and she had zero tolerance for boundaries. She would look into my phone and laugh at a video I'm playing or comment on a picture I'm looking at, she would always want to interfere when I'm talking to Jamie or his girlfriend, Arabella. Yes, Jamie and Arabella finally started going out a month ago and I'd never seen my brother so happy with any girl before. I was grateful for the relationship because it brought me closer to Arabella and the more I knew her, the more I loved her. But that's not the case right now.

Jennifer was smoldering me.

Hell, she even barged in one time when I was using the bathroom show me something on her phone and get me to choose between her purple thong or the lace panties. I felt like screaming that day and I still don't know how I told her to NEVER try such a thing again in such a calm and collected manner when all I wanted to do was scream and scream and scream.

"I'm sorry, Jennifer, we have to break up. I'm moving to California," I said one day as we ate Cheetos on my couch.

"Wait, what?"

"yeah, I got a job offer and I'm going to check it out. I don't know if I'm going to accept it and I don't know how long I'm going to stay in Cali."

Jennifer went "oh" and cried a little. She said that she understood and that I should take care of myself. It was true that I did get a temporary job offer from a firm in Cali.

Okay, Arabella hooked me up (another reason I loved that she was with my brother). She knew that I was into consulting and stuff and said that she had an uncle that was the member of the board of directors for a consulting firm in California. Her uncle Davey. I'm guessing she explained my situation and the man said that he would take me temporarily and after a month he'd decide if I'd make a valuable asset or not. If I impressed him, he'd give me three months of rigorous training and then a job. If not, it's bye-bye.

That bit was true, but I didn't have to leave for another three months. I just had to use it as an excuse right now because I was choking up!

Jennifer and I would often see each other in the building, but she's a smart girl, she figured out my drift. She didn't ask, "oh, you haven't left yet?" after the first time she asked and I mumbled something incoherent.

She had asked me if I was really going to Cali and I said that I was, just not immediately. She went "oh" again and slowly walked away. I felt a bit crappy. But I was grateful that she didn't create a scene or ask awkward questions or say vile things.

Well, that was that for Jennifer.

Chapter Twenty-Five

"Good morning, Miss Greenwood," Tammy Davis said cheerfully as I stepped into my office.

"Morning, Tammy," I said to the perky, blonde girl, "send my schedules for the day to my mail okay? I don't want any disturbance today till 1pm. I will be on a conference zoom meeting with some of our associates abroad and it will take a while because we are trying to bag a major deal. Please Tammy, see to it that I am *not* disturbed, is that clear?"

"Of course, ma. Perfectly understood," Tammy said and as I watched her efficient fingers fly over the keyboard with the speed of light, I knew that she would handle it.

Tammy Davis is the fourth P.A I've had and the best which is ironic because with her looks, I didn't expect much.

Yes, I know the "don't judge a book by the cover" thing but I can't help it and she looked like such an unserious, party, college student.

Safe to say that by her second week on the job, she had won me over. She was too organized, as sharp as a razor and she minded her business and faced her work.

I walked into my air-conditioned office and shut the door. I went to the little cupboard that was spacious enough to be used as a little closet and I kept my jacket in there. I checked to see that I had an extra suit and shirt. I had two, very good.

I went and sat at my disorganized desk,

Well, happy Monday morning, Kate.

I made to pick up the phone on my desk to tell Tammy to bring in coffee for me, but I heard a knock on my door.

"Come in."

And in came Tammy with a tray loaded with a jug of coffee, a cup, a spoon, a saucer of milk and another saucer of sweetener.

"Thank you, Tammy. I was just about to call but I should have known better, you know me as much as I know myself," I said.

And as usual, she had no reply but she did flush a little and I could see that my comment had made her really glad.

She makes the coffee just how I like it and after the first cup, I breathed in deeply. I was ready to tackle the day.

I checked the wall clock, the time was 8:27am. My meeting didn't start till 9:30am. I decided to attend to important emails and to go through the points I would be laying down during the meeting.

I was excited for the meeting. If all went through, we could have the trainers from McNolan Incorporated come train our new recruits.

McNolan Incorporated was one of the biggest training firms in USA and they had just opened a huge branch in California and having their professional trainer actually take out time to train your workforce and organize seminars and workshop sessions was like having all the answers to the question weeks before the exam. You automatically knew that your company will have twice more clients that it would usually have had if your staff hadn't been trained by the McNolan workforce.

We were trying to strike a long-term deal for the firm to be our trainers and it was like trying to strike a deal with God himself. But I had faith that we would get what we want.

I heard the phone ring.
"Hello?"
"Greenwood, my office now!"

I rolled my eyes and dropped the receiver. That would be my direct boss, always so dramatic.

Oh, I forgot to mention, I was the AGM (Assistant General Manager) of Whitewolf Consultancy; one of the biggest consulting firms in California.

Remember when I said that Arabella talked to her uncle about me and he said that he'd give me a trial? Well, he did give me a trial and that was six years ago.

I started as something less than an intern and now, I was the assistant general manager which was just in the name. Everyone knew that I had as much say as the G.M.

Hell, he even referred people back to me if they went to him directly.

Six years ago, I had come down to California; Bright-eyed, hungry and eager to learn. It wasn't easy, but I soaked up as much as I could during my one-month trial period.

On the day that my fate was to be decided, I faced a four-man board. I honestly thought that I'd be given the gate, but the outcome of that meeting still shocked me.

Uncle Davey (David Michelson) had said that I had impressed him beyond words could explain and the other men and woman in the board agreed.

Apparently, I was the smartest, most dedicated and most hardworking youngster that had had in a long while, if ever and they believed that if I could put the dedication and work that I put during that first month into my training to become a full member, I would be unstoppable.

And I did, oh how I did! I gave those three months everything I had and by the end of the three months, I was offered a higher job than the one I was promised.

That was how I started climbing the ladder, getting to where I am today and I had never looked back. It was a fun and exciting journey for me and I thanked Arabella every day in my mind.

Even though she and Jamie had broken up years ago, we still remained really good friends and what was more, she stayed in California too. She became my actual best friend a few months after I moved here and I realized that our destiny was to meet in college but our true friendship started growing the moment it was just us in California.

Just us, not hounded by a group. It was easy to become best friends. I mean, we already were in a clique!

I put thoughts of the past out of my mind as I hurried towards Wilbur's office.

I knocked and entered, "good morning, sir."

"Greenwood! Sit down, sit down, let me hear your idea for the bloody meeting today! We have to kill it and put it in a body bag, do you understand? I want all the Whitewolf staff that will be present in that meeting to body that meeting! We must get this contract."

I smiled and sat down, glad I had enough sense to come in with my notepad.

Now, let me tell you a little bit about Wilbur J. Manchester, Wilbur is a boss turned friend. He had been my direct boss for the past two years and I enjoyed working with him. Standing at 6 ft 5 and never appearing to calm down, with his too-tightly knotted tie and almost perpetually red face, he always looked like a volcano that was waiting to erupt.

A lot of staff feared him, they thought Wilbur was so scary and dangerous because of his booming voice and red angry face and hulking body, but he did nothing to me. I guess that's why he liked me so much.

When we first started working together, I showed him on the first week that I wasn't one to be easily intimidated. He yelled and bawled and complained about this perfect job I submitted and I put him in his place quietly. When we went through my submission together, he saw that he was the one that made the error and not me.

From that period, he had a certain type of respect for me and we got on just fine. I got to realize that the booming voice and volcano character were just who he was. That was how he got action. Underneath it all, he was a really loyal, hardworking and good boss who wanted nothing more than the success of the company and his staff.

Most of the staff were quick to discover that Wilbur treated me different and after they had discarded the rumors that we were sleeping together (he's married with three beautiful, strangely tall kids and I'm gay, duh), I became everyone's go to when some sensitive information had to be passed across to Wilbur. Because of this, the respect which I wasn't lacking in before increased dramatically and trust me, I loved every single moment of it. I loved excelling in my field.

Wilbur and I became friends when he suffered depression at one point. I'm used to staying late sometimes but Wilbur leaves by 5pm everyday like clockwork. I started noticing that at one point, he'd stay till 7pm or even close to 8pm. One day after I closed late (7:15pm), I was on my way to my car when I saw Wilbur crying in his car that was parked close to mine in the lot.

I don't know how but somehow, I got him to stop crying. In that moment of vulnerability, he told me everything. To cut the long story short, he had marital issues and his wife had moved into a hotel.

It took a while and some weeks but I gave him advice and one time I even had to meet his wife, Stella. Eventually, they worked out their issues but after that, I discovered that I had gained two new friends; Wilbur and Stella. They were really grateful to me, especially Wilbur. He had thought that me seeing him in that vulnerable state would affect how I saw him in the office or I'd go around blabbing about his issues to people. Eventually, he got to find out that I wasn't that kind of woman. It just wasn't me. And his respect for me increased drastically. When he discovered my sexuality, he liked me even more and he loved the fact that I could discuss women stuff both from a masculine (as a lover) and from a feminine point of view.

"Wow, Greenwood, just wow! You really are a ball of fire, aren't you? That was brilliant! If this doesn't stand those arrogant McNolan bastards on their ears, I don't know what will. That was brilliant," Wilbur beamed and rubbed his hands together. That was a sure sign that he was excited.

We discussed the meeting some more, discussed strategies and compared notes. By 9:20am, he shooed me out of his office to go get ready for the big meeting ahead. I crossed my fingers; I hope I kill it.

"Crush it today, ma'am," Tammy said, giving me a thumbs up as I hurried back to my office. I rushed into my office. I pulled off my tight black dress shoes and made another cup of coffee, took a deep breath and I was ready.

"Alright, everyone, have a great day ahead," I said as I hung up the connection. I checked the time, it was 12:44pm. What a long ass meeting.

I walked over to my door and announced to Tammy that I was done and that work could resume as usual. She asked how everything went and I told her that it was great. They'd get back to us in three days' time so that we can know if we had been awarded the contract or not. I tried not to think about it, fingers crossed.

***

Three days later, the tension in the office was so thick you could slice ham on it. Every single staff from the lowest rank to the highest rank knew about the McNolan deal and somehow, word had gotten around that today was the day we'd know our fate.

It wasn't that people talked or asked questions or stuff like that, not at all. It was just that the atmosphere was so charged in the office even if it was as quiet as a museum on Sunday night.

By 11, I was so tense that I could walk up the roof, but I forced myself to focus on the shitload of jobs I had on hand.

A bird I hand is worth three in the bushes. The contracts at hand are better than the McNolan contract we haven't yet received. So fucking focus on the ones you have! Make them good! Focus so as to not make errors, woman. Come on!

As I berated myself, I heard my phone ring,

"Greenwood, boardroom! Now!"

I didn't even take off my shoes when I came into my office. That's to show you how nervous I was. A regular me would have taken off her shoes the moment she walked into the office. These tight dress shoes kill me. They're sexy as sexy can be, but they kill me.

I walked to the boardroom and already, the general manager and his assistant of another one of our branches here in Cali were present. Slowly, the boardroom filled and when we were all seated, Wilbur stood. He looked almost larger than life and he seemed to expand in size as he bellowed, "we got the McNolan Incorporated contract!"

We cheered and from then on, it was all business talk about how we're going to go about the whole thing. Fee structures, pricing and everything were discussed.

To round up, Wilbur said, "it starts in two weeks. In two weeks' time, some of their trainers will come and inspect our facilities to know if there's anything necessary for our new recruits. They're the ones that will basically be in charge of the training because they're the ones running the branch of McNolan that opened up here in California. We have to make sure that everything goes as planned."

"Greenwood," he continued and when I looked at him to acknowledge my name, he said, "this project is in your hands. I know that you're a beast in handling such things so, the ball is in your court. You only report to me when there is a very important issue, okay?! And as for the rest of you, report to Greenwood. Do as she tells you. I'm swamped enough. Are we clear?"

We all nodded and after a little more chatter, we all dispersed.

"Greenwood, stay behind. I want to talk to you," Wilbur said as everyone filed out one by one until it was just the both of us.

"Now Greenwood, I trust you to handle this project. It is a big deal and if handled right, you get a commission of 1% on every new contract our newly trained recruits bring in for a duration of three months. That's a lot of money in your account, Greenwood. But that will only happen if all goes well."

I assured Wilbur that I wouldn't disappoint him. What he said made sweet music to my ears. A 1% cut for 3 months on every new deal brought in?! Even if it meant taking them to an actual military camp to train, I would do it! This money is enough incentive for me.

I walked back to my office, happy and ready for the challenge.

***

"Oh my gosh, that's pretty huge," Arabella said happily, drinking her margarita as I told her the good news, "McNolan Incorporated of all people! Wow Kate, you are the bomb."

"Girl, please. You know I wouldn't even be here without you, oh my gosh. I'm so grateful," I say, leaning in to squeeze my friend's hand.

Arabella rolled her eyes and swatted my hand, "I've told you to stop saying that."

We shared a laugh before I asked her, "so how's work? Is Ivan still driving you crazy?"

Arabella owned a gym. No, scratch that, she owned two gyms. She just decided a few years back that she had always been into fitness and wanted to operate her own gym. Money was never an issue for Arabella but I told her that she should start small and gauge people's reaction. I didn't want her spending a ton of money on equipment only for nobody to sign up. So, she started small, created a website and the website was what helped boost her business. It was an interactive one and people commented on what they'd actually like to see in a gym. Arabella used their comments to build her gym and after nearly two years of hard work, her gym was super successful and she had nothing less than 30 new members every month. I was so proud of her.

"Business is fine. You know I keep thinking I've met the craziest set of people when a new set of crazy people come along and totally floor me. So today,…"

She dove into one of her funny and crazy gym tale and by the time she was done, I wondered how I hadn't peed myself with laughter. While we talked though, my mind was on the contract I had landed. Fingers crossed.

Chapter Twenty-Six

Was I nervous? Maybe a little. Today was the day that the trainers from McNolan's would come to inspect our facilities. I noticed that I was more excited than nervous.

Finally, this was happening. But I willed myself to calm down. it wouldn't do well to be grinning and flitting around like an insect. I had to be professional.

They were due by 11am and before then, I was so engrossed in my work that I didn't even know when the time arrived.

The ringing of my phone startled me and when I put the receiver in my ear, Tammy's smooth voice told me that they had arrived and were waiting for me in the boardroom with Wilbur and some of the staff that were also in on the project.

I gathered my iPad, notepad and pen. I slipped my feet into my light brown loafers. I ran to my private bathroom to check myself out in the mirror and the face I saw looking back at me made me smile. I was ready.

As I walked to the boardroom, all ready to dive into the project, I had no idea that a huge surprise was waiting for me at the other side of the door.

I stepped into the board room and noted that three trainers came from McNolan Incorporated; two men and a woman. Their backs were to me as they were all shaking hands with Wilbur.

"Aha people, Miss Greenwood is here. Now, we can begin," Wilbur said to the trainers. Then to me, "Greenwood, come and say hello to the highly sought-after trainers from McNolan Incorporated. It's going to be a really wonderful and fruitful working relationship ahead, I hope,"

I was all smiles and as I was walked towards the trainers, they turned to see me and my heart stopped.

The woman amongst them was Marissa! That was Marissa freaking Evans!

My face must have changed color because I saw Wilbur shooting me a look that could freeze ice. I gathered myself together, but only just as we went on with the introductions. I didn't even hear the name of the men I introduced myself to first, I was only focused on Marissa.

I knew that she recognized me too because she had gasped when she turned around but she had collected herself quickly and as I shook her hand, her face was as expressionless as a hole in the wall.

"Hi, I'm Katherine Greenwood," I said, my heart almost hammering to death from the feel of her soft, warm hands in mine, it's funny how after twelve whole years, her hand still fit perfectly into mine.

"Marissa, Marissa Evans," she said coolly and snatched her hand away from mine. We all took our seats and the meeting began.

I was so glad that it wasn't a serious meeting and that I already knew what it was about if not, I would have been completely lost. It was all I could do not to stare at Marissa.

Damn, she was more beautiful than ever. It had been years since I saw her. It seemed like she just dropped out of sight. None of her social media accounts had been updated in five-six years, and here she was. In her Chanel pant suit and beautiful body. How is it possible that she gets more beautiful with age?

After the meeting, Wilbur instructed that I take them around our facilities for the inspection.

While we walked, I noticed that the men asked a few questions, but Marissa was mute. After the entire inspection, one of the men said, while Marissa walked around, looking at some of the equipment that had been checked before, "that will be all for now, miss Greenwood. Your facilities are not bad at all, they're up to date. However, there is some software that would need be installed and some other things that are highly necessary. But not to worry, miss Evans is our top trainer and will work in close quarters with you. She's a genius."

"Yes, miss Evans will be here for you. You just tell her your goals and visions for your recruits and let her work her magic."

Marissa had a ghost of a smile and after a while, they were all out. Safe to say that I didn't concentrate for the rest of the day. How could I? when Marissa and I would be working together three times a week for a month? And that was just the beginning of a 4-year long contract.

What have I gotten myself into?

***

"Tell me you're joking," Jamie said via the skype video call, "Marissa? *That* Marissa that you were crazy about in high school? Wow, what are the odds?"

James junior walked past the screen and I couldn't help but smile. He was so adorable and he was my nephew!

"Hey junior," I waved to the happy four-year-old who cooed and said, "heyyo, aunt Kay."

Jamie's baby mama, Chelsea, had dropped the baby off with Jamie when he was just a year-old, after visiting and saying she wanted to go get something from the mall. We never saw Chelsea again after that day and although it was tough at first, Jamie actually happened to be a wonderful father. James junior was a blessing because he made my brother more grounded, more responsible.

I could imagine the look on my mom's face had she been alive to hear that Jamie had a child out of wedlock. She and my father would have gone insane and probably disowned Jamie like they did me when I came out six years ago.

But they had both died in a car accident the same six years ago when they were hit by a drunk trucker.

It's sad losing both parents but asides from the natural rule which is unhappiness. I didn't miss them a lot or have any qualms that they passed on when we weren't on speaking terms. I hadn't seen them in years before the accident and they didn't care. They just never did.

Funny enough, they left all they had to Jamie and I. We split it equally and sold the house. We really didn't want to have anything to do with the house anymore and I was glad that Jamie and I were on the same page.

"Do I sound like I'm joking? She was there. Larger than life itself and looking me square in the eyes," I said transferring a large scoop of ice cream from the bowl to my mouth.

"Wow... this sounds like something out of one of them chick flicks or something. At least, tell me she aged fine?"

"Boy, she's fine-*er*! And I'm not joking. She more than aged well, she aged perfectly."

Jamie laughed and we talked about it. I told him about how nervous and distracted I felt and how it didn't even seem like she cared.

"I swear Jamie, she ain't look at me. Not even once. Like not even a glance. She was just seated there, as solid as a beautiful stone or an ice sculpture."

"But you know Marissa, Kate, she's mature and isn't one to throw fits or tantrums. If she was that mature at such a young age, imagine how she'd be now that she's an actual adult. She was a woman even before she became a woman so, ain't expect everything to be peaches and roses especially after the history that you both shared or, is you? And besides, why are we analyzing Marissa? Is there something you ain't telling?"

"We're analyzing her because I think I'm still in love with her, Jamie. Seeing her today just let this flood of emotions I didn't even know I had loose and I cried in my room."

After James finished laughing, he saw that I was glaring at him and quickly waved goodnight which was a good idea because I was ready to say some hurtful things to him.

I guess he read my mood. I was so frustrated.

I thought I'd gotten over this girl? This was since high school for fuck's sake.

As I laid in bed that night, images of Marissa clouded my reasoning. It's funny how some memories are stored somewhere in your brain and might not be retrieved for a long time. That night, so many memories of every little thing Marissa and I did together came flooding back into my mind. Even the ones I hadn't remembered before, little details came flooding back and I had to squeeze my pillow so hard.

Get a grip on yourself, Kate! You will be working with this woman now. How do you expect to work with her when your mind is in a turmoil? Never allow your personal issues affect your job! Nobody in the office cares what you're going through, just deliver. Everybody has their own shit. Most important thing is that you deliver when you have to, no excuses.

Even as I talked to myself, I knew that I had one hell of a battle ahead of me. And if I was going to win, I had to approach the matter delicately. I had to remind myself that this was a grown woman I was dealing with and not a teenage girl. A teenage girl who, by the way, was way too smart for her age then. As I drifted off into slumber, I hoped that I wouldn't dream about her.

Chapter Twenty-Seven

Marissa and I had been working together steadily for two weeks and she had been treating me like a total stranger. Just like a "colleague" which I technically was but then, it's crazy how I want her to just look at me with an expression in her eyes. Any expression. Anger, hatred, surprise, disappointment, anything!

But her eyes were as emotionless as wet stones. Her face was a blank cold mask and I hadn't had a moment with her alone in my office.

Today was going to be different though, she was going to tell me some of the things she had noticed and changes to be made. And she would do that…in my office with me, alone.

I hoped that she would loosen up at least, smile maybe but boy was I wrong.

She knocked and walked into my office by 9:30am prompt.

"Good morning, miss Greenwood," Marissa said as she walked to my desk, her heels making a sharp clicking sound on the ground.

"Hey, Marissa, good morning," I said.

This was the first time I'd called her "Marissa" and not "miss Evans" and if I was expecting a reaction from her, I didn't get it.

She just blinked at me and walked to the chair.

When she was settled in, she immediately dove into the work of the day. I wanted to talk about us…catch up, know how she's been but I decided that I should probably focus on work first.

Work before anything else. I told myself that as much as she was *my* Marissa, she was also one of the top trainers in McNolan Incorporated which was a pretty huge deal. A pretty, pretty huge deal.

We worked steadily for a little over two hours before we were finally done with what we had to do for the time.

When we were done, she started gathering her papers and notes.

"Um…could you stay for a while and talk?" I asked her as she shoved some documents into the pink file holder she carried.

"Is there a problem with the job?" she asked, looking a bit weary.

"Oh no, no. Not at all, the job is fine. It's not about the job at all, it's perfect," I replied and I saw that she relaxed into the chair.

"So, what seems to be the problem?"

"Could you just stop being so cold, Marissa? Stop treating me like a stranger, we know each other."

She cocked her head to one side and studied me as if I was a giant spider that crawled out of the ceiling, "do I know you? Do we really know each other? Listen to me, my dear, except for our names, we know nothing about each other. We are strangers."

"But that's not true and you know it. I mean we…we used to…in high school, we used to be…" I started to say and I was mortified to see that I couldn't breach that topic. I remembered the memories all too clearly.

"Because we were deceiving ourselves in high school that we were in love? That we were *together*? Please, grow up, Katherine. That was in the past. We were just a bunch of dumb delusional kids that just wanted to explore. It's been what? Twelve years? Just focus on the work. I'm not Marissa, I'm not Mari, call me miss Evans or Evans. And stop trying to be my friend. Stop trying to act like you want reconnect. That's a big pile of shit, just like the government saying they wanna change. Have a nice day, miss Greenwood," she retorted acidly and I was stunned to silence. Before I could think of what to say, she was already out the door and closed it with a soft click.

Marissa's words kept ringing in my head. I didn't want to believe that she meant all that she said to me but damn, it hurt. Did she mean what she said about us deceiving ourselves that we were in love?

So, all the while, it was never truly love for her? She was just playing with me?

I was suddenly consumed by anger. How could she even say such a thing? She's who had set my standards and expectations so high? She's who was the bar that every woman I dated had to fight to attain?

I decided that I'd give her space and watch her reaction.

If she stays away for real, then it means that she really doesn't want to have anything to do with me but if he gives a reaction, then it means a part of her still cares about me and that's what I want.

I gave Marissa the break. I started treating her exactly as she treated me, like a colleague. I did it for the first week, I did it for the second week but by the third week, I was already so exhausted. I just wanted her to talk to me! To laugh with me, to just be her most authentic self around me. But I guessed that I'd lost that part of her forever. I'd already-

My train of thought was interrupted by a knock on my door. Talk about the devil, it was Tammy coming to announce to me that Marissa wanted to see me. I told Tammy to send her in.

She walked into my office and I had to stop myself from drooling at the length and shape of her exquisite legs. Left to me, she should wear gowns for the rest of her life.

"Hey Greenwood, afternoon. I wanted to ask if you'd be interested in lunch?" she asked me and just like that, the ice was broken.

Marissa was her sweet self again, albeit more mature and reserved and so much smarter, she was still pretty much that girl. And after the lunch, it was easy to remember that before we actually started dating when we were younger, we found it easy being friends.

Three months in and Marissa and I were already "besties" in the office but was I in love with her? Yes, more than ever.

Now the question of the century is, how do I win her back?

Chapter Twenty-Eight

"Just calm down, Ivy. I'm sorry I didn't call you back for real. I've just been so swamped with work… but babe, you know I can't do that because work. Come on…" Marissa said in a soothing voice to her girlfriend, Ivy Lang over the phone.

Suddenly, the spaghetti I was eating became tasteless in my mouth. Marissa and I had been working together for about 10 months now and I was still jealous of Ivy Lang.

She and Marissa had started dating a couple of months before our contract was granted and hearing her speak to the quite cute Ivy (yes, I checked her on social media, sue me!) with that low, bedroom voice of hers got me so jealous.

Marissa and I were friends now, really friends. We even talked about our past relationship one time and Marissa admitted that I really hurt her feelings then.

I apologized and asked what I could do to make it right and she just smiled and waved her hand saying, "come on, Kate, it's been like decades, centuries even! Just let it rest, okay?"

But I wanted to make it right because the more I stayed with her, the more I fell for her.

She grew up a very wonderful woman and it was impossible for me not to love her. I had stopped all my college shenanigans of following different women every other month but I was still sexually active. At least, I had ladies that were down for a little roll in the sack with no strings attached but when Marissa came back into my life, it's like everyone disappeared.

I couldn't believe that I'd not had sex in close to 7 months! Me!

"Ivy wait… Ivy? Ivy?" Marissa sighed as she brought the phone down from her ear, "she hung up."

She sighed again and emptied her glass of vodka tonic in one swallow.

"Err, is everything okay?" I asked secretly delighted that everything was not, obviously. But I didn't betray that in my emotions. I hadn't made a move towards Marissa since we reconnected. I didn't want her to feel like it's all sexual. If anything did happen between us again, I wanted her to know that it was because of love. At least on my part.

"Really, no. Ivy has been acting up for days now and I'm really getting tired of her nagging. It's like she forgets that I work for one of the biggest corporations in the state. She's moving to New York, NY and wants me to come along with her. McNolan has good branches in NY but I love Cali! I love this new branch because I'm kind of the boss here and so far, it's been terrific. *This* is my domain. *This* is my territory. People are already heading to the NY offices, why can't she just understand that?"

Not knowing what to say, I just made supportive, cooing noises and waited. I knew Marissa so well. It was best not to say anything. I knew that she'd have more things to say before long.

"And I don't love her," she said after what seemed like a full five minutes, "I don't love her."

"But you're dating her?" I asked as casually as I could, aware that my heart was thumping wildly.

"Well, I'm fond of her and it just kind of happened. We met at yoga class at the gym and somehow became friends, you know? Then we just started hanging out and one day, we had sex. From there, we just sort of became a thing, you know? It was never truly defined and I thought I knew her really but getting to know her, damn. She is incredibly possessive and jealous as hell and really, I'm just exhausted."

She sighed and after a while, she said, "I'm sorry I'm yapping so much about my problems. I'd ask about your woman but we both know you're single."

"Hey, never apologize. What are friends for? If I don't listen to you, who will?" I asked, rubbing her palm.

I direct the conversation to work stuff to get her mind off Ivy. I didn't like the fact that another woman had such control over her emotions but at least, she didn't love her!

***

The moment Marissa stepped into the boardroom on Monday morning, I knew something was wrong. Her face was as hard as diamond and her eyes were like chips of ice. After the meeting, I told her to meet me in my office and not giving her a chance to argue, I walked to the my office quickly.

After a few minutes, Tammy knocked on my door and announced her in.

"What?" Marissa said the moment it was just the both of us.

"What's the problem, Mari? You're scaring me," I said half-jokingly.

She glared at me and said, "Ivy and I broke up on Saturday night. I just couldn't do it anymore and today, she's on her way to NY."

"Oh, I'm sorry," I said but I wasn't. I was ecstatic! I was on top of the world! Finally, the woman of my dreams was free!

"Then why do you look like Penny when you offer her a huge bowl of milk?" Marissa asked, crossing her arms and leaning against the wall.

I wanted to lie. I wanted to tell her that I didn't know what she was talking about but when I opened my mouth, what came out was,

"Because I'm glad. Marissa, I'm sorry your relationship crashed with Ivy but will I say I'm sad? No. and that's because I'm happy. I swear, I never stopped lovin- oh, fuck that. Just know that I'm not sad. I want to have you all to myself as much as I can."

Marissa's eyes grew wide and I expected her to say something but she just gulped and ran out of the office.

Way to go, big mouth! Way to go, freaking her out!

I sighed and pulled my laptop closer to immerse myself in my work. Maybe if I'm immersed in work, I wouldn't think about my fucking blunder.

I didn't see Marissa again till the next day and when I did, she acted normal. Like I didn't say all the revealing things I said and for that, I was grateful.

I didn't know how to start explaining myself to her or explaining what I meant or what I didn't mean.

I thought it would be awkward, but it really wasn't. She just smiled and was her usual self. She didn't even look like someone that just got out of a relationship. I thought she was putting up a front and expected it to slip at any moment, but it didn't.

I was glad to have her back and I was glad that she had forgotten about what I said, or so I thought…

***

"Another bottle of wine?" I asked Marissa as I stood up tipsily and headed to the fridge.

"Hell yes, another bottle of wine," she screamed.

We were celebrating.

A new set of recruits had completed their training today and today was a Friday. We decided to head over to my place after work to celebrate because I had told Marissa that I had a wine collection.

We had been to each other's houses a couple of times so, the request wasn't awkward or weird to her and she readily accepted.

We had arrived a little over an hour ago and had already downed one bottle of wine.

I got the second one and popped it and we squealed again.

Halfway into drinking the second bottle, Marissa kissed me right in the middle of a conversation. I didn't see it coming and I don't think she even thought it through. But one minute I was talking, the next minute, I felt her lips on mine and trust me, I immediately responded and lead the kiss. It was a deep kiss and all the memories we shared came crashing back as I wrapped my arms around her.

As if sensing that it was getting too personal, she pulled away and said, "I'm sorry, Kate I don't know why I did that. I guess the words you said to me that time Ivy and I broke up have been ringing in my head… I don't-I don't know why but they made me feel… good,"

She giggled and burped, she was a bit drunk but she knew what she was saying. It was like the liquor loosened her mouth. She talked and talked. A lot of things, I can't start to say but these are the words that burned themselves in my memory,

"I wanna have *that* talk now," she slurred, "I know you still like me. I see it in your eyes and I could too, but I don't trust you. You're a snake. You hurt me so badly, you have no idea. Before I learned to trust again, it was so hard. I was always waiting for the switch up or change that never came and it took me a long time to realize that all girls aren't like you. But you were my first and my realest. If I say that I don't still feel something for you, I'm lying but will I act on it? No, because you're… because.." she giggled, "because.. did I say because? Because you're a playerrrrrr!" she finally finished as she leaned into my soft cushions, sighing.

Her words cut through me like a knife and I decided that it was best we have the conversation when we're sober.

I took her to one of my spare bedrooms after we had a little argument which I won (I told her that I wasn't going to allow her drive home in her drunken state and she said she was fine). When I was sure she was okay, I slightly staggered back to mine and plopped into my bed fully clothed. I was out like a light in a few minutes and I knew she was too.

***

"Good morning, sleepyhead," I said as Marissa came into my kitchen as I was whipping us up some breakfast. She had just woken up and she looked so cute in the thick bathrobe I kept for her.

"Morning," she said as she stifled a yawn and stretched, "mmmm, that smells so divine. You got coffee?"

I directed her to the percolator and she poured herself a healthy amount of coffee with two spoons of sweetener, just the way she liked it.

We talked about this and that till breakfast was served.

After breakfast, I knew that she'd want to bolt but I didn't give her a chance, "about last night…" I began.

"It's cool, Kate I was drunk, pay no mind to me," she said, looking a bit flustered.

"We both know that drunk Mari is honest Mari but that's not the case. You got a lot of things off your chest. Now, it's my turn and you listen," that dom part of me kept her sitting still.

I started by telling her how much I missed her every day and how I know that I fucked things up. I told her about my sexual conquests in college and how I was unable to have a meaningful relationship because she set the bar too high.

When she made to interrupt, I shut her up by holding my finger up.

I told her how low I felt and how I always tried to look for her replacement. I told her about how I had to see a shrink a few years back after college and I told her the last truth,

"and I don't like you, Marissa. I love you and I will do anything to get you back. No matter how long it takes, I will win you back. And I'm for real this time. I've lost you once and I can't lose you again. Just don't shut me out, give me a chance to prove myself. Don't shy away."

She stood up and said, "I have to leave, Kate… but, I'll think about it."

Fingers crossed, please think about it!

***

"Marissa, will you marry me?" I asked on my knees, opening the little black box that contained a real diamond ring as she sat on the swing in her backyard.

She gasped and her eyes filled with tears.

While I waited for her response, I remembered how we got here.

It took a while and I had to exercise a lot of patience, but Marissa started giving me little chances to prove myself and I never shied away. I gave her everything I had; all my love, protection, care and I never demanded sex from her.

I wanted her to know that it wasn't about sex, instead, it was about her. She soaked up all my attention like a sponge and after a while, she started reciprocating.

But she wasn't that easy, little girl anymore and I had to constantly prove myself. She had deep trust issues concerning me and knowing it was my fault, I never grumbled when I had to do things to prove myself to her. I did it with love. And I loved the fact that we could separate work from pleasure, that was what turned me on the most about her. Her maturity.

We finally made love after four months of being together and I decided that night as she laid in my arms that I wanted to seal the deal with this lady.

I didn't think I could love anybody else this way and I didn't want to. I was content with just her.

I talked to Jamie about it and he gave me his full blessing. He had known about Marissa and I from the very beginning and they had even become friends over the course of our friendship and relationship.

Jamie loved her like a sister and he said that she was one of the smartest and most beautiful women he had seen in a while and that if I could get her, that was a jackpot.

So, I got the ring but I never found the courage to ask her to marry me.

I was sent on an official assignment to Paris and over there, I knew that I had to seal the deal immediately when I got back. We talked every single day and she was all I thought about aside from work. I knew that I had to wife her immediately before I went insane.

I had just gotten back from Paris a few hours ago (two days earlier than I told her, just to surprise her) and I knew she was home because we had been texting. I rushed over to my apartment to drop my bags and get her spare key, before I let myself into her house.

She almost died of excitement when she saw me and after hot quickie which we had right there on the floor of her sitting room, I told her to go out to the swing, that I got a little present for her from my trip.

Here was the present, the ring and there I was on my knees waiting.

"So... is that a yes or a go fuck yourself?" I asked, my heart pounding so loudly I thought she could hear it.

"Oh, yes! Yes! Yes!!" she said and as I slid the ring into her finger, she flung herself into my arms and we sealed our bond with a soul-stealing kiss.

It took me a long time, but what was mine finally came back to me. Not many people get a second chance, but I did. And although I worked so hard for it, I wouldn't have had it any other way.

As I held Marissa in my arms with my lips on hers and my ring on her finger, I knew that I had made the best decision I had ever made in my life.